PETER STEPHENS

THIRTEEN WITNESSES

TESTIMONIES ON THE PASSION AND DEATH OF JESUS CHRIST
AS THEY RELATE TO THE PURSUIT OF TRUTH

THIRTEEN WITNESSES

Testimonies on the Passion and Death of Jesus Christ as
They Relate to the Pursuit of Truth

A Fictional Work Based on Historical and
Scriptural Events

By Peter Stephens

Table of Contents

Dedication 1

Acknowledgements 3

List of Witnesses.. 5

Preface 7

Comment on the Gospel Accounts of the Passion and Death of Jesus:... 12

Background: Jesus Goes to Jerusalem to Complete His Ministry 14

The Judgment of the Nations (Matt 25:31-46) 16

Chapter 1: The First Witness – Alon.................................... 22

Chapter 2: The Second Witness – Betzalel........................... 28

Chapter 3: The Third Witness – Machla 33

Chapter 4: The Fourth Witness – Peter 38

Chapter 5: The Fifth Witness – Kaleb.................................. 44

Chapter 6: The Sixth Witness – Claudia 48

Chapter 7: The Seventh Witness – Decimus 56

Chapter 8: The Eighth Witness – Judas Iscariot................... 61

Chapter 9: The Ninth Witness – Veronica............................ 68

Chapter 10: The Tenth Witness – Simon of Cyrene 73

Chapter 11: The Eleventh Witness – Dismas 76

Chapter 12: The Twelfth Witness – Hannah 81

Chapter 13: The Thirteenth Witness – Lucius the Centurion 87

Chapter 14: Reflections on these Stories 95

Chapter 15: So What Does All This Mean? 105

Chapter 16: Conclusion.. 109

Chapter 17: Epilogue... 118

Appendix.. 123

Bibliography and Resources 128

Dedication

This book is dedicated to my late sister, Jewel FitzRoy Jacobs (1947 – 2023), whose life was a perfect example of a person who lived in the truth of Christ. Jewel was typical of all those nameless people in the world who actively engage in prayer, self-reflection, and meditation in an attempt to better understand themselves, their relationship to God, and how they should live their lives in this very complex world. These are the truth-seekers who do not pursue glory, status, or wealth because they are faithful enough, or naïve enough, to believe the truth will indeed set you free. These are the people who strive to attain perfection in their relationship with God and who understand intuitively, if not intellectually, that their example of love of God, love of each other, and love of self will help to improve this world, even if only in a minuscule way. They understand that changing the world first starts with changing yourself. To change yourself, you must first understand yourself, and for a Christian, there is no better way to do this than by sincerely meditating on the Scriptures – the life, death, and resurrection of Jesus Christ. By reflecting on these and other scriptural events, we can identify those weaknesses and faults within us that are obstacles to becoming what our Christian faith aspires us to be – an "alter Christus" – another Christ. Once this commitment is made, we then necessarily live up to that commitment through a life of service – service in the love of God and the love of community, a skill in which Jewel excelled.

Those of us who are Christian will more easily understand the benefit of meditating on the Passion and Death of Jesus Christ. However, the principles that love and truth are always superior to hate and lies in each and every situation are universal. These principles are espoused by all people – Christians, Jews, Muslims, Hindus, Sikhs, followers of Baha'ism, and non-religious persons, including atheists. Only those egotistical and self-absorbed deviants in our world, who are driven by greed and an unquenchable thirst for power, reject these principles.

In this social media-driven world, the blind acceptance of all that we hear and all that we are told is among the worst of sins because such unquestioning, robotic acceptance of information stifles our intellectual curiosity, prevents us from using critical thinking skills to seek "the good/the truth," and relegates us to a state of intellectual and moral slavery. When confronted with questionable "facts," we often do not ask: Is this true? Where is the evidence? What are the credentials and the legitimacy of the organization/person presenting these facts? Does it/he have an established reputation for truthfulness and for performing accurate and complete research? So many of us often choose to live in our protected cocoon of spurious facts rather than ask those difficult questions, because it is sometimes easier to live a lie than to pursue truth. This unthinking behavior is damaging not just to the individual but, if practiced by enough people, it is damaging to our communities and our society. Above all else, this book is about the search for truth. It concludes that Jesus Christ is the epitome of truth, and if one believes in the teachings of Jesus, he/she must pursue truth in all his/her endeavors. To pursue truth is to advocate belief in Jesus and to live the message of the gospels, to be the best "alter Christus" one can be. My sister Jewel was the best practitioner of pursuing these truths that I know.

Acknowledgements

T his book would never have been published if not for the support, encouragement, and constructive critique of family and friends. My late wife, Kathleen, whose patient tolerance of my procrastination is saintly; the four best children a father could ask for – Erica, Peter, Megan, and Nicole (Kinzer), all of whom provided support and encouragement when my self-doubt was rampant; my big brother, Ron, who looked after me as a child and still does so today; my little sisters, Jewel, who was the best Christian I know, and Marva, who thinks I am much better than I am.

Even rookie authors know that there is no perfectly written product initially produced from the imagination, improved through the lens of experience, that does not need the review and input of friends and professionals to make it better. *Thirteen Witnesses* is no exception, and I thank Fr. John Fernandes, who is retired and lives in Las Vegas, for making me go further than I originally intended; Katherine Sewell, my compatriot in working with adults who are interested in the Catholic faith through the Becoming Catholic program; Ron Brugada, another Becoming Catholic compatriot, who walked me through the publishing process; my old high school friend, Richard Giardina, for his very insightful comments in making the book more whole, more impactful, and a better reading experience; Bill Young, whose thoughts and questions forced me to look past the obvious; and Caleb Harms and Jeffrey Johnson, whose analysis of the characters and the theology was helpful and encouraging. And of course, every book is made better from the contributions of technical editors who have to do their work in spite of the author's ego. For their excellent work, I thank the editors of Amazon Publishing Company.

It should be noted that all direct biblical quotes from the New Testament are taken from the Revised Standard Version Catholic Edition of the New Testament, available at Bible Gateway (www.biblegateway.com). Quotes from the Book of Psalms and other Old Testament books are noted independently.

List of Witnesses

1. Alon – Male observer in the Garden of Gethsemane who witnessed Jesus' arrest. (Alon – means Oak tree; name originally given to a grandson of Jacob). Character and testimony are entirely fictional.

2. Betzalel – Priest, a member of the Sanhedrin who was present at Jesus' trial. (Betzalel – means "shadow of God"). Character and testimony are entirely fictional.

3. Machla – Woman who first accused Peter of being a disciple. (Machla – means "golden bangles" or "jewelry"). Character is mentioned in the Gospels; her name and testimony are fictional.

4. Peter – Disciple who denied Jesus three times. The details in his testimony that are not specified in the Gospels are fictional.

5. Kaleb (means whole-hearted, devoted, aggressive) – spice merchant in Jerusalem. A hard-core Pharisee who believes Jesus is a threat to Judaism and to Judea. He is a purely fictional character.

6. Claudia Procula – Pilate's wife, who had a premonition of what would befall Pilate if he condemned Jesus. Pilate's wife and her concern that Jesus was innocent are mentioned in the Gospel. Her name was first mentioned in a 4th-century document. Her testimony is entirely fictional.

7. Decimus – Roman soldier who scourged Jesus. (Decimus – means tenth). The scourging of Christ is mentioned in the Gospel; however, the name and the testimony of Decimus are entirely fictional.

8. Judas Iscariot – Disciple of Jesus who betrayed him. (Judas means "Praise"; Iscariot originally meant "one from Kerioth", later came to mean "traitor"). The details of his testimony that are not mentioned in the Gospels are fictional.

9. Veronica – Friend of Jesus' mother, Mary, and a follower of Jesus, who wiped his face when he fell the first time. (Veronica – means "true image"). This incident is not mentioned in the Gospel. The recount of Veronica helping Jesus is from Catholic tradition and the Catholic devotion "The Stations of the Cross". The testimony is entirely fictional.

10. Simon of Cyrene – Foreigner who was drafted to help Jesus carry his cross after he fell the third time. Character is mentioned by name in the Gospels; however, his testimony is fictional.

11. Hannah – Sympathetic mother supporting Mary (Hannah – means "favor" or "grace"). Shares her feelings as a mother as she supports Mary in her time of grief. Character and testimony are entirely fictional.

12. Dismas – The Good Thief, who recognizes Christ's innocence and gets immediate forgiveness and conversion. (Dismas – means "sunset" or "death"). Character is mentioned by name in the Gospels; however, his testimony is fictional.

13. Lucius (Lucius – means "light") – Roman Centurion who was present for the entire proceedings against Jesus and who supervised the crucifixion. It was he who recognized that truly this man was the Son of God. Character is mentioned only as a Centurion in the Gospels. His name and testimony are fictional.

Preface

Christians all know the story of the trial, passion, and death of Jesus Christ. Without His death, there would have been no Resurrection. Without His Resurrection, there would be no Christianity, since His Resurrection proved once and for all that He is the Son of God and that His death and resurrection are the keys to our renewed relationship with God and to our salvation. Christians believe the Resurrection is the seminal event in salvation history and is the single most important event in secular human history. Most people, even non-Christians, know the story all too well. It is recorded in the four Gospels, which we hear very often in church, and the Passion, Death, and Resurrection, or elements of it, are subjects in visual and performing arts, including painting, sculpture, literature, plays, and movies.

The Gospels give a very complete account of the passion and resurrection of Jesus Christ, but for many people, it is not entirely clear why He was executed. We know what happened to Jesus, and we know how it happened. We know who His enemies were. We know the ones who attacked Him; the ones who gave false witness about Him; the ones who were jealous of who He was, and why they thought He was a threat to them. Why was Peter's fear so great that he denied knowing Jesus? Why did Judas betray Him? And why were there no clear and specific reasons for His condemnation? A trial requires a finding of guilt or innocence, and if guilty, then judgment is passed by a lawfully approved authority. Yet Jesus' judge, Pontius Pilate, said he found no guilt in this man. This singular fact frustrated Pontius Pilate so much that he simply gave in to the mob because there was no reasoning with them, even when crucifixion for the crimes allegedly committed by Jesus was not justified under Roman law (Matt 27:1-26). On the fringes of the allegations against Jesus is the question of truth – who is He? John 18:37-38 reads: Pilate asked Him, "So You are a king?"

Jesus answered, "You say that I am a king. For this I was born, and for this I came into the world, to testify to the truth. Everyone who belongs to the truth listens to my voice." Pilate asked Him, "What is truth?" (John 18:37-38) Jesus did not respond.

There are so many more people involved in the story of Jesus' death that the only way to get more insight into this story and to get an understanding of who He was and the truth He espoused is to hear the testimony of those present, including participants, disciples of Jesus, spectators, and those who obeyed the orders to scourge and crucify Him. We know His disciples were present, with Peter and Judas being the two most prominent. There is Caiaphas, the High Priest; Pontius Pilate, the governor of Judaea; Roman soldiers; the nameless members of the crowd that followed Him; the unknown persons in the mob that screamed for His death; the Roman soldier who flogged Him; Simon of Cyrene, who helped carry His cross; the women of Jerusalem who cried for Him; a "good" thief and a "bad" thief who were crucified with Him, and the Centurion who supervised His crucifixion. We know all this, but did we ever stop to think about how these lesser players and witnesses felt about the events of His passion and death? Who were they? What insights did they have? What kind of people were they? Were some of them kind, loving, and compassionate, while others were malicious, selfish, or indifferent? What did they believe about Jesus? Did they buy into the lies of the Pharisees and the conspiracies they concocted? And most importantly, do their testimonies add any clarity to who the man Jesus was? This book hopes to answer these questions by giving you a fictionalized insight into these players – what they heard and saw, what they thought, and how the Crucifixion event impacted them.

Essentially, this is a book about thirteen people whose lives were irrevocably changed, for good or ill, as a result of an encounter they had directly or indirectly with Jesus Christ during his passion, and the decisions they had to make to accept or reject the truth of his divinity. It is a book that validates the journey in life we all undertake and how our lives can be enriched by events when we care enough to ask ourselves difficult questions, and not passively let these events pass us by. We are enriched by these events, become better people, as we honestly and humbly evaluate them, asking ourselves pertinent questions so that we can have a better understanding of what we are seeing and experiencing. It is a book that encourages personal reflection on our lives as we continue on our daily journey, and our responsibility to pursue truth regardless of the consequences. It is hoped that the reader will have a better understanding of the value of truth, and that belief in falsity, especially falsity created to protect the power of the leadership in the status quo, eventually leads to tragedy and disaster, as in the case of Jesus – the execution of an innocent man.

The most important purpose in reading this book is to stimulate the reader to perform acts of personal reflection on the Passion and Death of Jesus Christ by reading, and "living" the testimony of the thirteen witnesses. Each witness' testimony is a heavily fictionalized perspective as imagined by the author. While some of the witnesses were real people mentioned in the Gospels, e.g. Peter, Judas, Claudia - wife of Pontius Pilate, Simon of Cyrene, Dismas and the Roman Centurion, other witnesses are completely fictionalized. The story of each witness is also fictionalized, some more than others. The story of each witness is faithful to the gospel accounts to the degree that the gospels tell us about the individual person or the collective group that the person represents. It is my hope that the reader will, at some point, engage in his/her own reflection on these events, by becoming a fourteenth witness if you will, using these stories as a starting point.

We should not underestimate the learning that results from acts of personal reflection. The act of reflecting, and ultimately meditating - i.e. listening to God when He speaks to our hearts - is what increases our understanding of these events; it is what gives insight to ourselves and identifies the areas in which we need to grow; and it is what gives us the grace to grow spiritually and to develop a personal relationship with Him.

The story told by the witnesses follows the Passion of Christ in a linear fashion as written in the Gospels of the four evangelists - Matthew, Mark, Luke and John, using direct quotes from the New Revised Standard Version, Anglicized Catholic Edition (NRSVCE) translation of the Bible. These quotes are interspersed in appropriate places with fictionalized testimony to give the reader an understanding of what participants and eyewitnesses of these events may have seen and how those events may have affected their thinking and their belief. Certain facts in the testimony of the witnesses are taken from the Gospels and other scriptural sources and Catholic religious tradition when such facts are relevant to the testimony of a specific witness. Although most of the testimonies will have portions that are based on scriptural sources, the majority of the testimony of each is fictionalized.

It is hoped that the telling of the testimony of these witnesses will bring, as vividly as possible, to the reader's imagination the horror of the physical suffering of Jesus, but to do so in the imagination and not by any extensive description of the torture and pain that he suffered. However, that is not the most important purpose of the book. The most important purpose is for the reader to expand his/her understanding of the passion and death of Jesus Christ to include the social, political and mob forces at work and to get insight into Jesus' response to these events and how understanding his response is a most valuable lesson for us in how we should live our lives and how we can grow in our personal spirituality. Ideally, readers will put themselves in the person of each witness and question whether the witness' response to the events experienced was reasonable, appropriate, and/or understandable. Then the readers should go one step further and imagine themselves as witnesses seeing and hearing what these witnesses saw and heard and explore within themselves what they would have thought and what they would have done.

Comment on the Gospel Accounts of the Passion and Death of Jesus:

We have specific and detailed information about the events leading to the passion of Christ. The Synoptic Gospels (Matthew, Mark, and Luke) are remarkably consistent in explaining these events, and they do so in very direct, specific, and sterile terms. John also includes the majority of these events, but he focuses more on Jesus' teaching and the moral (theological) lessons He has for His disciples and for us, resulting in a much deeper and richer explanation of Jesus' passion. The Synoptic Gospels are very similar in recording the events in Jesus' life, though some are more expansive than others, from the time that the conspiracy against Him first began, to the entry into Jerusalem, the Last Supper, the Agony in the Garden, His arrest, Peter's denial, Jesus' trial by the Sanhedrin and again by Pilate, His scourging, sentencing to death, crown of thorns, carrying of His cross, crucifixion, death, and Resurrection.

As mentioned, John includes the majority of these events; however, his recording of these events is much richer, with much more moral teaching and greater insight into the forces at work that resulted in the crucifixion. For example, John includes events and discourses by Jesus that are not recorded in the Synoptics. These include the washing of the disciples' feet; the new commandment of love—to love one another as I have loved you; extensive discourses at the Last Supper, including the prediction of the coming of the Advocate; the discussion that He is the vine and we are the branches; the warning that we must be prepared to be hated by the world; and an extensive prayer in which He gives everything the Father gave Him to the apostles and to those who believe in Him. After His resurrection, John records Jesus' appearance to Mary Magdalene, His discourse on faith with Thomas, and His discourse with Peter to "feed My sheep."

It is not the purpose of this book to go into any detail on these discourses and teachings of Jesus, as they would deviate from the stated purpose of evaluating the testimony of the thirteen witnesses. For those who have not done so, I encourage you to read the Gospel of John, specifically Chapters 12 – 21, to gain a much deeper understanding of Jesus' passion and death and the moral lessons He taught to the apostles.

Background: Jesus Goes to Jerusalem to Complete His Ministry

Jesus is at the end of His ministry of preaching and healing. He is on the way to Jerusalem for the Passover, which was a very normal thing for a Jew to do. Although He knew what would happen to Him in Jerusalem, and after He had given His disciples several strong hints, even direct statements, that He would die and be resurrected, they still refused to believe Him. He was their raison d'être, and they would not allow thoughts of His death to destroy, or so they believed, everything they had tried to build under His leadership. Until the events of Pentecost (when the Paraclete comes upon the apostles in the form of tongues of fire), the disciples were convinced that their purpose, their mission, was gone, no longer possible. With Jesus dead, there was no hope; there was no way they could continue without His presence, His guidance, and His leadership.

To fully understand the Passion of Jesus Christ, we must start with the events preceding His triumphant entry into Jerusalem. We must have some idea of His person, why He was hailed as a king, and why that fact was important in His trial. Matthew begins his account with the Judgment of Nations, in which Jesus explains what will happen when the Son of Man comes in glory with all His angels and separates the goats from the sheep, the bad from the good, the virtuous from the sinners. Then events quickly take a turn for the worse as the plot to kill Jesus takes root. After Jesus is anointed by Mary in Bethany (a prefiguring of His death and burial), He enters Jerusalem to cheers of

Hosanna, after which His status deteriorates rapidly as the plan to arrest and kill Him begins to unfold.

To have a more complete understanding of the Passion and Death of Jesus Christ, especially the reasons for it, one must first understand the events in Jesus' ministry immediately preceding His arrest. These events give meaning and insight into the man, His mission, and the reasons why He was hated by the established Jewish hierarchy. These events begin with the Judgment of Nations and end with Jesus praying in the Garden of Gethsemane. In order to not filter or interpret these events in any way, I am quoting them verbatim from the New Revised Standard Version, Anglicized Catholic Edition (NRSVACE) for you to read and interpret for yourself. The testimony of each witness is preceded by a direct quote from the New Testament that is relevant to that witness' belief, behavior, and final decision regarding the guilt of Jesus.

The Judgment of the Nations (Matt 25:31-46)

When the Son of Man comes in His glory, and all the angels with Him, then He will sit on the throne of His glory. All the nations will be gathered before Him, and He will separate people one from another as a shepherd separates the sheep from the goats, and He will put the sheep at His right hand and the goats at the left. Then the King will say to those at His right hand, "Come, you that are blessed by My Father, inherit the kingdom prepared for you from the foundation of the world; for I was hungry and you gave Me food, I was thirsty and you gave Me something to drink, I was a stranger and you welcomed Me, I was naked and you gave Me clothing, I was sick and you took care of Me, I was in prison and you visited Me."

Then the righteous will answer Him, "Lord, when was it that we saw You hungry and gave You food, or thirsty and gave You something to drink? And when was it that we saw You a stranger and welcomed You, or naked and gave You clothing? And when was it that we saw You sick or in prison and visited You?"

And the King will answer them, "Truly I tell you, just as you did it to one of the least of these who are members of My family, you did it to Me."

Then He will say to those at His left hand, "You that are accursed, depart from Me into the eternal fire prepared for the devil and his angels; for I was hungry and you gave Me no food, I was thirsty and you gave Me nothing to drink, I was a stranger and you did not welcome Me, naked and you did not give Me clothing, sick and in prison and you did not visit Me."

Then they also will answer, "Lord, when was it that we saw You hungry or thirsty or a stranger or naked or sick or in prison, and did not take care of You?"

Then He will answer them, "Truly I tell you, just as you did not do it to one of the least of these, you did not do it to Me." And these will go away into eternal punishment, but the righteous into eternal life.

The Plot to Kill Jesus (Matt 26:1-5)

"When Jesus had finished saying all these things, He said to His disciples, 'You know that after two days the Passover is coming, and the Son of Man will be handed over to be crucified.' Then the chief priests and the elders of the people gathered in the palace of the high priest, who was called Caiaphas, and they conspired to arrest Jesus by stealth and kill Him. But they said, 'Not during the festival, or there may be a riot among the people.'"

The Anointing at Bethany (John 12:1-8)

Six days before the Passover, Jesus came to Bethany, the home of Lazarus, whom He had raised from the dead. There, they gave a dinner for Him. Martha served, and Lazarus was one of those at the table with Him. Mary took a pound of costly perfume made of pure nard, anointed Jesus' feet, and wiped them with her hair. The house was filled with the fragrance of the perfume. But Judas Iscariot, one of His disciples (the one who was about to betray Him), said, "Why was this perfume not sold for three hundred denarii and the money given to the poor?" (He said this not because he cared about the poor, but because he was a thief; he kept the common purse and used to steal what was put into it.) Jesus said, "Leave her alone. She bought it so that she might keep it for the day of My burial. You always have the poor with you, but you do not always have Me."

Jesus' Triumphal Entry into Jerusalem (John 12:12-19)

The next day, the great crowd that had come to the festival heard that Jesus was coming to Jerusalem. So, they took branches of palm trees and went out to meet Him, shouting: "Hosanna! Blessed is the one who comes in the name of the Lord — the King of Israel!" Jesus found a young donkey and sat on it, as it is written: "Do not be afraid, daughter of Zion. Look, your king is coming, sitting on a donkey's colt!" His disciples did not understand these things at first; but when Jesus was glorified, then they remembered that these things had been written of Him and had been done to Him. So, the crowd that had been with Him when He called Lazarus out of the tomb and raised him from the dead continued to testify. It was also because they heard that He had performed this sign that the crowd went to meet Him. The Pharisees then said to one another, "You see, you can do nothing. Look, the world has gone after Him!"

Judas Agrees to Betray Jesus (Matt 21:14-16)

Then one of the twelve, who was called Judas Iscariot, went to the chief priests and said, "What will you give me if I betray Him to you?" They paid him thirty pieces of silver. And from that moment, he began to look for an opportunity to betray Him.

The Passover with the Disciples (Mark 14:12-21)

On the first day of Unleavened Bread, when the Passover lamb is sacrificed, His disciples said to Him, "Where do You want us to go and make the preparations for You to eat the Passover?" So, He sent two of His disciples, saying to them, "Go into the city, and a man carrying a jar of water will meet you; follow him, and wherever he enters, say to the owner of the house, 'The Teacher asks, Where is My guest room where I may eat the Passover with My disciples?' He will show you a large room upstairs, furnished and ready. Make preparations for us there." So, the disciples set out and went to the city, and found everything He had told them; and they prepared the Passover meal. When it was evening, He came with the twelve. And when they had taken their places and were eating, Jesus said, "Truly I tell you, one of you will betray Me, one who is eating with Me." They began to be distressed and to say to Him one after another, "Surely, not I?" He said to them, "It is one of the twelve, one who is dipping bread into the bowl with Me. For the Son of Man goes as it is written of Him, but woe to that one by whom the Son of Man is betrayed! It would have been better for that one not to have been born."

The Institution of the Lord's Supper (Luke 22:14-23)

When the hour came, He took His place at the table, and the apostles with Him. He said to them, "I have eagerly desired to eat this Passover with you before I suffer; for I tell you, I will not eat it until it is fulfilled in the kingdom of God." Then He took a cup, and after giving thanks, He said, "Take this and divide it among yourselves; for I tell you that from now on I will not drink of the fruit of the vine until the kingdom of God comes." Then He took a loaf of bread, and when He had given thanks, He broke it and gave it to them, saying, "This is My body, which is given for you. Do this in remembrance of Me." And He did the same with the cup after supper, saying, "This cup that is poured out for you is the new covenant in My blood. But see, the one who betrays Me is with Me, and His hand is on the table. For the Son of Man is going as it has been determined, but woe to that one by whom He is betrayed!" Then they began to ask one another which one of them it could be who would do this.

Peter's Denial Foretold (Mark 14:26-31)

When they had sung the hymn, they went out to the Mount of Olives. And Jesus said to them, "You will all become deserters; for it is written: 'I will strike the shepherd, and the sheep will be scattered.' But after I am raised up, I will go before you to Galilee." Peter said to Him, "Even though all become deserters, I will not." Jesus said to him,

"Truly I tell you, this day, this very night, before the cock crows twice, you will deny Me three times." But he said vehemently, "Even though I must die with You, I will not deny You." And all of them said the same.

Jesus Foretells His Betrayal (John 13:20-30)

Very truly, I tell you, whoever receives one whom I send receives Me; and whoever receives Me receives Him who sent Me." After saying this, Jesus was troubled in spirit, and declared, "Very truly, I tell you, one of you will betray Me." The disciples looked at one another, uncertain of whom He was speaking. One of His disciples—the one whom Jesus loved—was reclining next to Him; Simon Peter therefore motioned to him to ask Jesus of whom He was speaking. So, while reclining next to Jesus, he asked Him, "Lord, who is it?" Jesus answered, "It is the one to whom I give this piece of bread when I have dipped it in the dish." So, when He had dipped the piece of bread, He gave it to Judas son of Simon Iscariot. After he received the piece of bread, Satan entered into him. Jesus said to him, "Do quickly what you are going to do." Now, no one at the table knew why He said this to him. Some thought that, because Judas had the common purse, Jesus was telling him, "Buy what we need for the festival"; or, that he should give something to the poor. So, after receiving the piece of bread, he immediately went out. And it was night.

Jesus Prays in Gethsemane (Matt 26:36-46)

Then Jesus went with them to a place called Gethsemane; and He said to His disciples, "Sit here while I go over there and pray." He took with Him Peter and the two sons of Zebedee, and began to be grieved and agitated. Then He said to them, "I am deeply grieved, even to death; remain here, and stay awake with Me." And going a little farther, He threw Himself on the ground and prayed, "My Father, if it is possible, let this cup pass from Me; yet not what I want but what You want." Then He came to the disciples and found them sleeping;

and He said to Peter, "So, could you not stay awake with Me one hour? Stay awake and pray that you may not come into the time of trial; the spirit indeed is willing, but the flesh is weak." Again, He went away for the second time and prayed, "My Father, if this cannot pass unless I drink it, Your will be done." Again, He came and found them sleeping, for their eyes were heavy. So, leaving them again, He went away and prayed for the third time, saying the same words. Then He came to the disciples and said to them, "Are you still sleeping and taking your rest? See, the hour is at hand, and the Son of Man is betrayed into the hands of sinners. Get up, let us be going. See, My betrayer is at hand."

Chapter 1
The First Witness – Alon

"This above all, to thine own self be true" William Shakespeare, Hamlet, Act I.

The Betrayal and Arrest of Jesus (Luke 22: 47-53)

While He was still speaking, suddenly a crowd came, and the one called Judas, one of the twelve, was leading them. He approached Jesus to kiss Him; but Jesus said to Him, "Judas, is it with a kiss that you are betraying the Son of Man?" When those who were around Him saw what was coming, they asked, "Lord, should we strike with the sword?" Then one of them struck the slave of the high priest and cut off His right ear. But Jesus said, "No more of this!" And he touched His ear and healed Him. Then Jesus said to the chief priests, the officers of the temple police, and the elders who had come for Him, "Have you come out with swords and clubs as if I were a bandit? When I was with you day after day in the temple, you did not lay hands on me. But this is your hour, and the power of darkness!"

The Testimony of Alon:

My name is Alon. I am a Jew, and a weaver by trade. I was born and raised in Ekron, west of Emmaus in Judea. I moved to Jerusalem 15 years ago so that I could purchase the wool, yarn, and cotton I use in my business from the traders who came from North Africa, Ethiopia, Egypt, Syria, and points East to do business in Jerusalem.

Some merchant friends of mine told me of an incident in the temple in which the man named Jesus became angry at merchants for conducting business in the temple area. Apparently, He acted like a madman, knocking over stalls and yelling at vendors. When it was over, He calmly received several of the poor who had serious illnesses or disabilities, and He cured them all. When He interacted with them, he gave them words of encouragement and support that noticeably uplifted their spirits.

Cured? I asked. How can He cure a person instantly who has been sick for years? And what words did He say to lift the spirits of such poor and desperate people? They could not answer my inquiry except to say He must have been from God. From God or from the evil one, I asked myself. Whoever this man was, I found the reports of His behavior intriguing. Who can be so bold and audacious to attack Jewish merchants in the temple, thoroughly reprimanding them, then calmly heal the sick? This was the first thing He did that challenged my thinking and made me want to understand who He was.

The thought of what He did with such passionate conviction that He was right would not leave me, so I started asking others about Him. I found out he was a preacher who supposedly had healed many people of illnesses, could even drive out demons, and preached that the Pharisees and leaders of the synagogues did not know and did not care about God's love, that they were hypocrites who loved status and power more than they loved God. As a follower of the Pharisees, I found this teaching extremely offensive and destructive to our traditional beliefs which we embraced and defended. Again, I believed He could not be from God, because God could not, would not, send someone to tear down what He had taught us from the time of Moses and what He had inspired us to build. I put Him out of my mind and did not pursue any further inquiries because there were a lot of people out there preaching that they were the Messiah or that they were prophets from God, and we should follow them because they knew what God wanted from us.

I was ready to rid my memory of Him because He was just another charlatan, when I heard that the Sanhedrin was going to arrest Him and have Him tried by Pontius Pilate for treason against Rome. This really intrigued me as I wondered what did the Sanhedrin know. Based on what He did in the temple area, maybe He was a rabble-rouser; maybe He even destroyed some personal property, but treason? Against Rome? I was mystified. No one I knew could tell me anything to clear up the confusion. Then I heard that the arrest would take place two days before the Feast of the Passover, which for me was a very inconvenient day, as my family is so heavily involved in Passover preparation for family coming in from distant regions. But I was so intrigued; I knew I had to be there when He was arrested, and when He was tried. I had to hear the charges and His defense. I had to know what this man was about.

On the Thursday before Passover, I went to the house of Caiaphas the High Priest, where the Sanhedrin held their meetings. A sizeable crowd, some armed with makeshift weapons, had already gathered, and there were individuals in the crowd speaking very negatively of the man Jesus, accusing Him of blasphemy and treason, and saying He was an agent of the devil. The crowd was becoming agitated and very quickly was becoming a mob. About 3:00 PM, a man came through the gate, whispered to the guard who was there, and was escorted into the building to the High Priest's office. I did not know who that man was, but from his dress, it was obvious he was a Jew, and not from Jerusalem. I later found out his name was Judas. After several minutes, he came out on the portico with Caiaphas and members of the Sanhedrin. Caiaphas called the leader of the temple guard, told him something, and he quickly called for a squad of guards to come to him. The guards lined up in two columns and followed their leader and Judas as they left the courtyard and went through the gate. Rumors started spreading immediately that they were going to arrest Jesus, and so most of the crowd followed the soldiers and Judas. Against all logic and good sense, I decided to join them and followed with the crowd.

We walked for about a mile and entered an undeveloped area with trees and bushes called Gethsemane. After going in a little way, we saw four men about 150 yards ahead. As we got closer, Judas ran up to them and kissed the one called Jesus, whom I could now see and recognize, and greeted Him, calling Him Rabbi. Jesus said something in return which I could not hear, but I could see His demeanor was calm and His voice was soft. Then, suddenly, in a desperate effort to defend their master, one of His followers surprised one of the guards by pulling his sword from its sheath and, with a swift blow, severed the right ear of the High Priest's servant, who happened to be in the front and the one closest to the assailant. I struggled hard to get closer to the front of the crowd, which was difficult as no one would make way for me. Fearing a violent response to this attack, I saw Jesus calmly replace and heal the ear of the servant, and as I struggled to get closer, I heard Him say words that cautioned against violence, that those who use the sword will die by the sword. I was close enough to see His face clearly. It was serene and filled with compassion. Why was He not afraid? The guards seemed to respond in kind as one guard on each side of Him held Him by the elbow and led Him a few feet away from the crowd.

Here was a man about to be arrested and to be tried by the Sanhedrin for crimes I certainly did not understand, nor believe that He had committed. And yet He is healing the injured and teaching about non-violence. This was the second thing He did to challenge my thinking.

Jesus engaged in conversation with those before Him, all of which I could not hear. As I got a bit closer, I heard Him ask: "Day after day I sat teaching in the temple area, yet you did not arrest Me?" My question exactly! Why had they not arrested Him before if His preaching was treasonous? This was the third thing He did to challenge my thinking. I was becoming very uncomfortable with my thoughts about the legitimacy of the accusations against Him and the honesty of the Sanhedrin in alleging He was guilty of crimes that required a formal trial.

As I watched His interaction with the guards and with Judas, and listened as much as I could to His words, I detected no fear, no anger, and no outrage at His being arrested. Even when His followers slipped away from the guards and ran away, I heard no complaint, no pleading to not desert him. There was no resistance in word or action; just a very quiet acceptance, almost as if He was being compliant to a fate He did not wish to evade. This really concerned me because it was so unusual. I have seen people arrested before, and I have never seen anyone take it so calmly, so casually, and so serenely, because the thought of going to a Roman prison was not a pleasant one. In my relatively short life and limited experience with judicial proceedings, this was not normal, and this was the fourth thing He did to really challenge my thinking. I do not know exactly who this man was, but I do know he was different; He was not of the norm of us. I know some in the crowd said He was a prophet, a man of God. I do not know if that is true, but I must admit, I saw nothing to reject that theory and everything to advance it.

As we returned to the house of the high priest, my head was filled with conflicting thoughts about this man. I could not summarize His actions and put them neatly in a box that said, yes, this is a bad man; He must be tried under penalty of death for His crimes. I instinctively knew what the outcome of His trial would be and decided I could get the particulars of his trial from others. I decided to return home with the hope of reflecting on all I had seen and experienced that day and, with a new perspective, hopefully get some understanding. I could not help but think that what was happening to this man did not make sense, that He was innocent of those charges.

My deliberations were to no avail, as I could come to no clear conclusion on who this man Jesus was. It was not long after His death that word was spreading that His followers were preaching in the streets; that they said He was the Son of God, and He was resurrected from the dead. As outlandish as this seemed, I could not forget the behavior of Jesus, what He said, and what he did under the most extreme situations of stress. I remembered the man I saw and decided I must go to hear for myself what His followers were preaching; just possibly they might be able to explain to me who He was, help me to understand why He did what He did, and hopefully clarify the conundrum that filled my mind.

Chapter 2
The Second Witness – Betzalel

Jesus before the High Priest (Matt 26:57-68)

Those who had arrested Jesus took Him to Caiaphas the high priest, in whose house the scribes and the elders had gathered. But Peter was following Him at a distance, as far as the courtyard of the high priest; and going inside, he sat with the guards in order to see how this would end. Now the chief priests and the whole council were looking for false testimony against Jesus so that they might put Him to death, but they found none, though many false witnesses came forward. At last, two came forwadrd and said, "This fellow said, 'I am able to destroy the temple of God and to build it in three days.'" The high priest stood up and said, "Have you no answer? What is it that they testify against you?" But Jesus was silent. Then the high priest said to Him, "I put you under oath before the living God, tell us if you are the Messiah, the Son of God." Jesus said to him, "You have said so. But I tell you, From now on you will see the Son of Man seated at the right hand of Power and coming on the clouds of heaven."

Then the high priest tore his clothes and said, "He has blasphemed! Why do we still need witnesses? You have now heard His blasphemy. What is your verdict?" They answered, "He deserves death." Then they spat in His face and struck Him; and some slapped Him, saying, "Prophesy to us, you Messiah! Who is it that struck you?"

The Testimony of Betzalel:

My name is Betzalel. I am a Levite, a Sadducee, and a member of the Sanhedrin. I am a colleague of Caiaphas the High Priest and was a member of the tribunal that tried the case of the blasphemer Jesus in Jerusalem just before Passover. The Sanhedrin is a council of specially selected men well-versed in the Law of Moses and acts as the judge and jury regarding all religious and civil crimes committed by Jews in Israel. The largest of the Sanhedrin Councils, called the Greater Sanhedrin, is the highest Jewish Court in the land and it is located in Jerusalem. It consists of 70 members, men of status and respect, and is led by Caiaphas, the High Priest; and I had the honor of being one of them.

It was the Thursday before the Passover celebration when Annas, serving as the High Priest of the lesser Sanhedrin, held an informal review of the case of Jesus, who was accused of blasphemy. After this initial hearing, Annas referred Jesus to the Greater Sanhedrin for a formal trial concerning the crimes of which He was accused. Jesus was presented to the Greater Sanhedrin and Caiaphas, who was Annas' son-in-law, during the late afternoon hours, about 5:00 PM.

As the council was convened, Caiaphas addressed the accused Jesus, telling Him the charges against Him. The charges were enumerated one by one: (1) Blasphemy against God and the people of Israel by claiming to be the Son of God; (2) Lying to the people with outrageous statements, saying He can rebuild the temple in three days; (3) Frequently disobeying the Law of Moses regarding interaction with sinners and working on the Sabbath; (4) Acting as a teacher and Rabbi when He has no authority to do so; (5) Being an agent of the devil since He has no authority to perform signs from God, therefore His authority must be from the devil; (6) Treason against Rome by claiming to be the King of the Jews.

Jesus walked into the council chamber, with three guards, each to His left and His right. He walked to the front and stood before the High Priest. His tunic had blotches of dirt on it, and His face was bruised with slight traces of blood on his lower cheek, below his lip. At this point, His injuries were slight, probably inflicted when He was arrested or taken to the Lesser Sanhedrin.

Caiaphas addressed the assembly, telling them of the charges against Jesus. Jesus did not respond either in word or facial expression. His eyes were focused, but I could see neither fear, nor anger, nor disdain for the people attacking Him, nor for the proceedings. My best guess is that He had come to a point of acceptance of His fate and that He was being consistent with what I later found out He had taught – one must always love, even those who hate you.

The council brought witnesses to testify. Several made claims against Him, all of them accusing Him of assorted crimes against the Law of Moses and of the customary traditions of the Jewish people, but none of them were clearly seen to be significant religious crimes or legitimate criminal charges against the laws of Rome. Things got very exciting when Jesus finally spoke, responding to a very excited and angry Caiaphas who demanded to know if He was the Messiah. Jesus responded but did not give a clear "yes" or "no" answer. He said something about us seeing the Son of Man seated at the right hand of God and coming on the clouds of heaven. At first, I was unsure if He was referring to Himself as the Son of Man; but once I had that understanding, after everyone on the Council became incensed with this outrageous statement, I too became very angry and shouted with the others that this was the height of blasphemy. The emotion in the room was raw; the response of the crowd was loud to the point of being deafening; and, as I reflect on it, it was like being in a chariot in which the horses were galloping at full speed down a hill and you had lost the reins and could not slow them down. They just pulled you along and you were powerless to stop or to change direction.

Caiaphas and most of the Council fed the anger of the crowd and inflamed things more by saying Jesus had condemned Himself. As the crowd responded to the Sanhedrin's condemnation of Jesus, it began to erupt in words and actions against Him. Caiaphas then screamed out, "What should we do with Him?" Even though I was still feeling extreme anger against Jesus, I was surprised the crowd overwhelmingly responded, "Kill Him! Kill Him!" Even in the heightened emotional state I was in, I was very surprised at the passion and the unanimity of this response because I did not believe this was a capital offense. I did not know how we had gotten to this point so quickly. It was not until the following day that I discovered that several members of the Sanhedrin had planted provocateurs in the crowd to make these responses at the appropriate time so that they could manipulate the crowd's anger. If the anger is sufficiently ugly, it would be a positive factor for them when they referred Jesus to Pontius Pilate, because more than anything else Pilate did not want a riot in the streets as that would be a very black mark on his leadership and limit further opportunities for him with Rome. Everyone knew Pilate was all about personal glory. Caiaphas knew very well he did not have the authority to execute. Only the Roman governor could do that, so he had to find a way to make Pilate his ally, and he had to give Pilate enough reason – or enough fear – to have him make the "right" decision.

Once the mob started screaming, many turned on Jesus, temporarily overpowering the guards, hitting Jesus with whatever was handy, and spitting on Him. The guards slowly regained control, and Caiaphas ordered Jesus to be taken to Pilate for trial, though I was still unsure about the charges that could be brought against Him to Pilate, who was an agent of Rome. Now, Jesus was more visibly bruised, with His tunic torn and more blood visible on His face; but His eyes had not changed. It still had that hard-to-define look that I interpreted to mean, "You can kill Me, but you cannot break Me."

After going home and reflecting on the events I had seen and participated in, I attended Jesus' trial before Pilate at the Praetorium. To my mind, the very worst thing Jesus was guilty of was heresy against Jewish beliefs and the Law of Moses. I could not understand how His passion for His beliefs, and even his ranting and raving as a preacher, could be considered an act of treason against Rome. After watching Pilate try several times to give Jesus a way out, it seemed to me that Pilate also did not believe Him guilty of treason. Even though I had questions about His guilt, I knew that once Pilate capitulated to the crowd, giving them the opportunity to select Barabbas as the one to be released, Jesus' fate was sealed, and He would be executed. Even though I saw no evidence that he was guilty of treason, and I believed the inevitable death sentence He would receive would be unjust, I was obligated to support the Sanhedrin. I could not be the only one not to support the Council's decision, as such a failure to do so would subject me to condemnation by my peers, probable expulsion from the Sanhedrin, and public rejection of me in my role as a religious leader. Furthermore, such support on my part for Jesus would not have changed anything, as He would still be sentenced to death. I am not now, nor was I ever, fully comfortable with this final position I took; but I justified my decision because I was convinced that Jesus was a threat to our beliefs and the Mosaic Law; consequently, He must die. I suppressed the objections that were growing in my chest and kept quiet.

Chapter 3
The Third Witness – Machla

Peter Denies Jesus (Mark 15: 60-72)

While Peter was below in the courtyard, one of the servant-girls of the high priest came by. When she saw Peter warming himself, she stared at him and said, "You also were with Jesus, the man from Nazareth." But he denied it, saying, "I do not know or understand what you are talking about." And he went out into the forecourt. Then the cock crowed. And the servant-girl, on seeing him, began again to say to the bystanders, "This man is one of them." But again, he denied it. Then after a little while, the bystanders again said to Peter, "Certainly you are one of them; for you are a Galilean." But he began to curse, and he swore an oath, "I do not know this man you are talking about." At that moment, the cock crowed for the second time. Then Peter remembered that Jesus had said to him, "Before the cock crows twice, you will deny Me three times." And he broke down and wept.

The Testimony of Machla:

My name is Machla. I am 23 years old. I was born in Hebron, and my family has been in Palestine for 150 years. I moved with my family to Jerusalem when I was five. My family is originally from Parthia, which is located between the Tigris River and the Caspian Sea, to the distant Northeast of Palestine. We left Parthia during the invasion of the Seleucids and relocated to Palestine. Even though I speak Greek and Aramaic, and some Hebrew, I am still considered to be a foreigner by most Jews since I am not descended from the Israelites, so the only job I could get is that of a servant in the kitchens of the High Priest Caiaphas.

I usually do not get involved in politics or in the business of the Jews, but on that Thursday afternoon, when the crowd came to Caiaphas' house, complaining to Caiaphas about a man named Jesus, I was curious, so I joined the crowd to see what the fuss was about. I did not understand what the issue was, only that the people were all stirred up about this man Jesus because of things He had said or done. After a while, another man joined them. He seemed to have information that they wanted, because the Sanhedrin sent this man with soldiers out to do something. Some of the crowd followed, and so did I. I soon found out that they were going to arrest the man Jesus because He was a blasphemer and was insulting their God.

When we got to the place called Gethsemane, we saw the soldiers approach four men in conversation, sitting a short distance away. For some reason, my interest was really piqued, so I struggled to get as close as I could to the front of the crowd in order to see and hear what was going on. As the soldiers approached them, the four men stood up, and it was easy to see who was the leader. The man called Jesus stood in the front with his three allies behind and to his left and his right, in a half circle behind Him. Jesus was taller than the others, wearing a soiled cotton tunic that went below the knee; a woolen mantle was draped around His shoulders. His sandals were open-toed and well-worn. His hair was uncombed, and His beard was scruffy and ill-kempt. There was nothing distinguished about His appearance, but His demeanor was quiet and serene. With His reputation for being a great scholar, and for His fearlessness in challenging civil authority, I certainly expected a person of some stature, if not in size, at least in appearance. The only thing I noticed that was different, even special, were His eyes. It was not their size or their color that attracted my gaze; it was the clarity of their expression, one that communicated understanding, compassion, and fearlessness.

As He spoke with the soldiers, I looked at His companions. Like Him, the three of them were inconspicuous. Their dress was similar, equally poor, and equally tattered and dirty. They were lean and disheveled, with the look of hard-working men, somewhat malnourished, yet still energized in movement and action. As best as I could tell, they ranged in age from about 25 to 35, the youngest one also being the smallest. Two of the men, including the younger one, seemed to defer to the third man, who was broad-shouldered with muscular arms and a fuller beard than the others. He had the look of a hard-working laborer, a farmer, or a fisherman. This man, whom I saw clearly, used hand gestures to restrain the other two as they got excited about something the soldiers said. Suddenly, this man pulled the sword from one of the soldiers and lashed out at one of the servants accompanying the soldiers, cutting off his ear. At this point, I expected an explosion from the soldiers, that they would respond in anger and with violence, even possibly killing the four men they were facing. But that did not happen. Jesus said something I could not hear, but His words seemed to have a calming effect on them. Then He bent over, picked up the servant's ear from the ground, and reattached it to the side of His head. Later, I looked at that servant's ear and I could not detect even a scar. It was like it never happened. I am still mystified.

As we started to walk back with the prisoner, I suddenly noticed His three friends were gone. I did not see them leave; it seemed as if they just vanished. After the walk back to the Sanhedrin, I was in the courtyard area since I could not get into the room, and was standing close to a fairly large fire that had been set since darkness was approaching and the temperature was dropping. There was a lot of shouting in the room, and you could hear "Kill Him! Kill Him!" so I knew it was not going well for Jesus. As I watched the response of those in the courtyard, most of whom agreed with the comments coming from the closed room. Then I saw him – the broad-shouldered, muscular one who accompanied Jesus and who cut off the ear of the soldier. He was fairly close to the fire, close enough for warmth, not close enough to be uncomfortable. He was standing by himself, his mantle wrapped around his chin, looking down very dejectedly, but most of his face was exposed. That face, those shoulders, and those arms – definitely it was he, the accomplice of the one called Jesus.

I went up to him and confronted him, saying in all certainty that he was with the one who was arrested, the man called Jesus. He looked up at me with a painful and hurt expression on his face and said firmly, "No, that I was mistaken." His lie angered me, so I raised my voice, saying with even more certainty: "Surely you are one of His followers." He got even more excited and walked very quickly out the main gate, wanting to get away from me as quickly as he could. I recall this incident frequently, as I often ask myself why he was in such a dejected state. Why did he lie? What was the man Jesus to him? Was it just a master-servant relationship or something more? Why could he not go to the Sanhedrin and speak on Jesus' behalf? If he were scared of being arrested, why did he follow Him to the Sanhedrin? The behavior of this man alternately supported and rejected His master. I found both behaviors interesting and confusing to ponder, but I never did get any answers.

I saw this man only once more, several weeks after these events, and found out his name was Peter. He was in Jerusalem, preaching about Jesus Christ, whom he said was the Messiah, the one he had denied and who the Jews crucified. He preached openly and loudly with Roman and religious guards all around him, yet he had no fear. Their presence almost seemed to embolden him. He was not the same person I saw the night his master was being tried. I asked myself, how can this be the same man who ran from a girl who accused him of being a friend of Jesus? Now he is screaming to the world that he is not only a friend of this man who was condemned by the Sanhedrin and by Pilate but also a disciple, appealing to all who would listen that salvation is possible only through belief in the man Jesus, the one they hung on a cross. His fearlessness was astonishing to the point of being foolish. I could not understand such a transformation, but it made me want to know more about what he was preaching. Any belief that could give a man – an alleged coward – such confidence and courage was a belief I wanted to evaluate for myself. It was not long after that I joined a group of believers and attended many gatherings in which Peter and his colleagues taught us about the man Jesus, what He did, what He believed, and why He was the Son of God. As I listened to their preaching, the solemnity and the sanctity they expressed when they spoke of the teachings of Jesus and His message of love, I could feel the veils of cynicism, distrust, and even hate peel from my inner being. As I began to see clearly, my heart warmed as I embraced this message of love, and I willingly joined the community of believers. Once I came to this belief, I chose to be baptized by Peter.

Chapter 4
The Fourth Witness – Peter

Peter Denies Jesus (Luke 22: 54-62)

Then they seized Him and led Him away, bringing Him into the high priest's house. But Peter was following at a distance. When they had kindled a fire in the middle of the courtyard and sat down together, Peter sat among them. Then a servant-girl, seeing Him in the firelight, stared at Him and said, "This man also was with Him." But He denied it, saying, "Woman, I do not know Him." A little later, someone else, on seeing him, said, "You also are one of them." But Peter said, "Man, I am not!" Then, about an hour later, still another kept insisting, "Surely this man also was with him; for he is a Galilean." But Peter said, "Man, I do not know what you are talking about!" At that moment, while he was still speaking, the cock crowed. The Lord turned and looked at Peter. Then Peter remembered the word of the Lord, how He had said to him, "Before the cock crows today, you will deny Me three times." And he went out and wept bitterly.

The Testimony of Peter:

My name is Simon, son of Jonah, and I am a fisherman from Galilee. My brother Andrew and I were casting our fishing net into the Sea of Galilee when Jesus walked by and said, "Follow me, and I will make you fish for people." I cannot explain why we did so, but Andrew and I immediately left our net and followed him. From that moment, we became His disciples, and not long after, He renamed me

Peter. It is very difficult for me to explain the relationship I had with Jesus; and it is even more difficult to explain why I denied Him, not once, but three times. I am a Jew, a very traditional Jew, who believes strongly in the Law of Moses. I am a native of Galilee, and I am a fisherman by trade. I am both a good Jew and a good fisherman. I am married and have two boys who will be fishermen, and also one girl who will marry a fisherman.

Andrew and I have discussed our initial meeting with Jesus several times, and we still do not know why we left our nets and followed Him. The best explanation I have is one that Andrew gave; it is helpful but not fully complete. Andrew said that, when he heard Jesus' invitation, it was as if all the burden of work that he had been feeling had lifted away. His feet became light and energized; his heart leapt from his chest; and his mind became very clear and very focused on this man. Andrew is much better with words than I am, and I must admit I felt all of those feelings also. The one thing Andrew left out is that I had a feeling of hunger, of wanting more of what this man had to give.

For me and for the other eleven who lived with Him and traveled with Him, He was much more than Master, Teacher, and Rabbi. He took us to a place of learning and understanding that was way past the Mosaic Law and the teaching of the prophets. He gave us an understanding of God's mercy and God's love that was nowhere to be found in the sacred writings or in the teaching of the Pharisees. It was through the love He showed everyone with whom He interacted, whether they were lepers or sinners, rich or poor, possessed or lame, that we came to understand how much He loved each and every one of us individually, regardless of our virtues or our vices. By living with Him for three years, witnessing miracles that still leave me speechless, and being a part of everything He did, and by listening to every word He said, He made us want to be like Him in everything we did or said. Yet we knew that we could not fully measure up to his standards. Still, He never gave up on us; he continued to guide us, to show us, and to encourage us, even when we did not understand Him, which was actually quite often. To say we admired Him, respected Him, obeyed Him, loved Him, and absolutely came to believe He was the Son of God, only makes it more difficult for me to explain, and for you to understand, my sin in denying Him, not once but three times.

I often jumped to conclusions, causing Jesus to correct me, but there was one time when my answer was correct. Jesus asked me, "Who do you say that I am?" And without thinking, the answer came to me in a flash, and I responded, "You are the Messiah, the Son of the living God." Jesus gave me a very strong blessing and said that my name was now Peter, and I would be the rock upon which He would build His church. I did not understand what that meant until after His resurrection when we were filled with the Holy Spirit and had the courage to preach in His name, converting Jews and Gentiles.

I remember the events of those three days of torture, crucifixion, and resurrection very clearly. It is like they are branded in my memory the way some Roman soldiers are tattooed to identify the unit to which they belonged. We had finished our Passover meal during which Jesus did some very unusual things. Most notable of all was the blessing and sharing of the bread and wine, and His command to us to continue to do this in His memory. Confusing to us was when Jesus accused Judas of his intent to betray Him; and Judas offered no denial, instead, he left our company to do what He had to do as Jesus commanded him. It was upsetting and disconcerting; but we did not know exactly what it meant, and we were too afraid to ask, because a betrayal by one seemed to be a betrayal by all. After the meal, Jesus asked James, John, and me to accompany Him to the place called Gethsemane, where He would pray. As Jesus prayed, the three of us fell asleep, since we were very tired from the week's activities. Suddenly, Jesus woke us up and told us that His betrayer was coming. In a few minutes, Judas appeared with soldiers, followed by a crowd. Here was a cherished friend, companion, and colleague approaching us; but he never acknowledged us and went directly to Jesus. As he reached

Jesus, he kissed Him, addressing Him as Rabbi. Immediately, the soldiers took hold of Jesus; and suddenly, in a rush, I understood the cryptic sayings Jesus had made about His death and I realized that this moment had come. Without thinking, my immediate response was to fight, to protect Jesus, so I grabbed a sword from one of the soldiers and struck at them, resulting in one of the attendants losing his ear. Already, I had forgotten His fundamental teaching about violence. He healed the servant with the severed ear, looked at me with those eyes that communicated repudiation, compassion, and forgiveness all at the same time, and admonished me for the use of violence. I knew that once again, my impulsiveness was a problem.

The soldiers surrounded Jesus, ostensibly to protect Him from the crowd, and started marching Him back to Jerusalem. James, John, and I looked at each other, having no idea what to do. We instinctively understood that this was a pivotal moment, not just for Jesus, but for all of us; and if He could be arrested and taken to the Sanhedrin, then so could we. As the crowd turned to follow the soldiers, the three of us slipped away, went in the opposite direction to where there were more trees and vegetation, and hid.

After the crowd disappeared, we talked about what we should do. James and John wanted to return to the place where we had eaten the Passover meal, which I must admit was the smart thing to do. But, of course, I disagreed and decided to go to see Jesus' trial by the Sanhedrin. James and John tried to dissuade me because they obviously knew the much increased probability of being seen and possibly arrested, but I was adamant. John decided to come with me (to protect me, I think), and James returned to the room of our last meal. John and I followed the crowd at a distance to the house of Caiaphas, where the trial was being held. Of course, I had completely forgotten Jesus' prophecy that tonight I would deny him three times. I believe I forgot Jesus' words because, even when Jesus spoke them to me, I completely discarded them. For once, He was wrong, I thought; there is no way I would or could deny Him. But I did. Not once, not twice, but three times. Three times I was a coward; three times I was so consumed by fear for my miserable life that, in those brief moments, I rejected all that I believed, all that I was, all that I wanted to be. How was that possible? How could I have rejected Jesus, after all that I had seen Him do, all that I had heard Him say, all those times I sat at His feet and tried to consume His words and His teaching, and in my heart striving to be like Him? How was it possible that all that was no longer a part of me and that I was able to say, "No, I do not know the man!" My God, My God, what have I become?

I remember the moment of the third denial. Jesus was restrained and the guards were taking Him to be scourged. He was about twenty feet away from me as He was passing by, well within earshot. Someone again accused me of being one of His followers; and like the previous two times I denied it, but this time with emphasis and expletives. Jesus heard and looked at me, and I looked at Him, for just a brief moment. Then the cock crowed, and His prediction of my denial came rushing into my consciousness, as did my instinctive and arrogant response that I would die for Him rather than deny Him. The reality of those words and the reality of my denial were more than I could bear. A burden of disgust, self-rejection, and personal disbelief of my cowardice came upon me, and the only response I had was to run away. I ran, and ran, and ran some more. In my shame and sorrow, it seemed that somehow, no matter how untrue, the farther I got away, the lesser was my sin, the more tolerable was my pain. I later found myself kneeling under a tree with my head on a rock, crying in a manner I had never done before. My sorrow grew as I recalled the look on Jesus' face when our eyes met at my third denial. If only it were a look of anger, of total repudiation, or even of "I told you so," I would have felt better. Instead, it was a look of understanding, of forgiveness, and of love. How could He continue to love one as despicable as me? My chest heaved with sobs. Tears came not just from my eyes but from my very soul, and I am sure my cries for forgiveness were heard throughout the breadth of the universe.

I do not know how long I was there, but it was several hours. When my very troubled soul reached a level of calm, I was able to reflect within myself, to stop beating myself, and to ask myself, what must I do for forgiveness? It was then that I was filled with the grace of God as I remembered the words of the 51st Psalm:

Have mercy on me, O God, in your kindness,
In your compassion, blot out my offense.
Wash me more and more from my guilt,
and cleanse me from my sin.
A pure heart create for me, O God,
Put a steadfast spirit within me.
Do not cast me away from your presence,
Nor deprive me of your holy spirit.

Give me again the joy of your help;
With a spirit of fervor, sustain me,
That I may teach transgressors your ways
And sinners may return to you.

O rescue me, God, my helper,
And my tongue shall ring out your goodness…
My sacrifice a contrite spirit,
A humbled, contrite heart you will not spurn.

I will never know for certain exactly what saved me, until that time when I am face to face with Jesus, who has promised to come again. But I do know that I did not have the strength, the energy, and the purpose of life to pick myself up from under that tree and return to face my brothers in the room where we had last eaten, until after I had repeated that Psalm out loud and in my heart many, many times and received the grace of forgiveness.

Chapter 5
The Fifth Witness – Kaleb

John 2:13-17

The Passover of the Jews was near, and Jesus went up to Jerusalem. In the temple, He found people selling cattle, sheep, and doves, and the money changers seated at their tables. Making a whip of cords, He drove all of them out of the temple, both the sheep and the cattle. He also poured out the coins of the money changers and overturned their tables. He told those who were selling the doves, "Take these things out of here! Stop making my Father's house a marketplace!" His disciples remembered that it was written, "Zeal for your house will consume me." (John 2:17)

The Testimony of Kaleb:

My name is Kaleb. I am a merchant. I sell fragrances and spices that come from Antioch, Egypt, Syria, and Arabia for personal use and for cooking. I am a Jew, a follower of the Pharisees, and committed to obeying the Law of Moses. My family has lived in Jerusalem for almost 200 years, from before the Maccabean Revolt against the Seleucids, who wanted to convert the Jewish people to Greek idolatry. My ancestors fought with Judas Maccabeus and his brothers Jonathan Apphus and Simon Thassi. We won that war and drove the Seleucids out of Jerusalem because of the power given us by the one God, the God of Moses. I will not tolerate anyone who brings dishonor to

Yahweh, who does not honor our traditions and our belief in the Law of Moses.

I know of this man Jesus. He is a Jew from Galilee, and I believe He is a traitor to all Jews and to our religious heritage. I first heard of Him when He stopped a crowd from stoning an adulterous woman to death. The Law is clear; an adulterous woman is punished by stoning to death. Who is this man, a raggedy preacher, to pervert the justice taught to us by Moses and the prophets? I am told that, after He embarrassed the men in the crowd with word trickery, they left, and He then spoke with the woman and told her He did not condemn her. He does not have the right to not condemn her because that is the Law. I condemn her, and if I had been there, I would have thrown many stones.

My friends have told me what they have heard Jesus say and what they have seen Him do. He fraternizes with sinners; He eats with them and stays in their houses. He engages with lepers and many others of the unclean and does not practice our ritual cleaning. He himself does not obey the Law to not work on the Sabbath, and He says it is acceptable for others to not do so also. He freely engages in discourse with women without their husbands or fathers present. He rejects our belief that the pain and suffering in our lives is the result of personal sin and the sin of our ancestors, and He tells the poor and the unwanted that their lives are important to God, and they will be one with God. Everyone knows His so-called healing is a sham and that He pays people to say He healed them from afflictions they never had. He even has a tax collector, the most despised of characters, as one of His followers. And maybe worst of all, He tells stories that show that Samaritans are superior in morality to Jews. This man is a threat to the sanctity of our laws, to our relationship with God, and to our very way of life.

When I heard that He was arrested and was to be tried for treason, I was overjoyed. I hurried to the Praetorium because I wanted to see and hear everything that would happen at His trial. I heard the witnesses against Him, and their testimony only increased my anger at Him. When one witness stated that He said He could rebuild the temple in three days, I was furious at such arrogance. Finally, when Caiaphas asked Him if He was the Son of God and He answered that we will see Him at the right hand of God coming down from heaven, I could no longer control myself. When Caiaphas, in total frustration, asked what we should do with Him, I heard someone scream, "Kill Him," and some moments later I realized that someone was me. Others quickly joined in, and we began to chant, "Kill Him; Kill Him." Some of the crowd closest to Him punched Him and hit Him with objects, but I was not close enough to do so, although I would have gladly done so. After Caiaphas sent Him to Pilate, I joined the crowd and followed because I was much too invested in seeing this man fully punished to walk away. I watched and listened as Pilate seemed to do as much as he could to have Him released with little or no punishment, which angered me and most of the crowd. When Pilate tried his last desperate attempt to free Jesus, and asked to whom he should grant a pardon and release in accordance with Roman law, I and the crowd responded in unison, "Barabbas, Barabbas." Pilate was visibly shaken, as this was a response he did not expect, because Barabbas was a proven villain, a murderer, and a threat to public safety. As bad as Barabbas was, Jesus was worse because He threatened the very foundation of our society, the basis of our relationship with God. When Pilate asked what he should do with Jesus, I again led the chant, "Crucify Him." Pilate hung his head in defeat and gave Him to us.

I followed the soldiers back to the courtyard of the Praetorium, where the soldiers began the process for execution by crucifixion. I watched the scourging, the placing of the crown of thorns on His head, the carrying of the cross to Golgotha, the nailing of the hands and feet, and finally the erection of the cross. I must admit, I was pleased with these events, as I believed then, and still do now, that this man deserved to be stopped and to be punished in a most powerful way for His blasphemous acts against God. The only thing that disappointed me was that at no time did I hear Him scream in pain, beg for mercy, or show any remorse. For the blasphemous charlatan that He was, I can only say he seemed to have the courage of His convictions.

Upon His death, reports were made of some unusual events that occurred. There was an earthquake, but that is not unusual in Judea. The fact that it happened at the moment of His death was just a coincidence; and earthquakes cause damage, which this one did to the temple. Wild reports of the dead being resurrected were simply His followers making up stories to prove that He was special to God. This man was a liar and a charlatan, a man who presented Himself as someone special from God, and He was not; and His followers are committed to perpetuating that lie. He was a threat to our way of life, to our traditions, to our beliefs in the Law. His punishment was justified.

Chapter 6
The Sixth Witness – Claudia

Jesus before Herod (Luke 23:6-12)

When Pilate heard this, he asked whether the man was a Galilean. And when he learned that he was under Herod's jurisdiction, he sent Him off to Herod, who was himself in Jerusalem at that time. When Herod saw Jesus, he was very glad, for he had wanted to see Him for a long time because he had heard about Him and was hoping to see Him perform some sign. He questioned Him at some length, but Jesus gave Him no answer. The chief priests and the scribes stood by, vehemently accusing Him. Even Herod, with his soldiers, treated Him with contempt and mocked Him; then he put an elegant robe on Him and sent Him back to Pilate. That same day Herod and Pilate became friends with each other; before this, they had been enemies.

Jesus before Pilate (John 18:28-38)

Then they took Jesus from Caiaphas to Pilate's headquarters. It was early in the morning. They themselves did not enter the headquarters, so as to avoid ritual defilement and to be able to eat the Passover. So, Pilate went out to them and said, "What accusation do you bring against this man?" They answered, "If this man were not a criminal, we would not have handed Him over to you." Pilate said to them, "Take Him yourselves and judge Him according to your law." The Jews replied, "We are not permitted to put anyone to death." (This was to fulfill what Jesus had said when He indicated the kind of death he was to die.) Then Pilate entered the headquarters again, summoned Jesus, and asked Him, "Are you the King of the Jews?" Jesus answered, "Do you ask this on your own, or did others tell you about Me?" Pilate replied, "I am not a Jew, am I? Your own nation and the chief priests have handed you over to me. What have you done?" Jesus answered, "My kingdom is not from this world. If my kingdom were from this world, my followers would be fighting to keep Me from being handed over to the Jews. But as it is, my kingdom is not from here." Pilate asked Him, "So you are a king?" Jesus answered, "You say that I am a king. For this I was born, and for this I came into the world, to testify to the truth. Everyone who belongs to the truth listens to my voice." Pilate asked Him, "What is truth?"

Barabbas or Jesus? (Matt 27:15-20)

Now at the festival, the governor was accustomed to releasing a prisoner for the crowd, anyone whom they wanted. At that time, they had a notorious prisoner, called Barabbas. So, after they had gathered, Pilate said to them, "Whom do you want me to release for you, Barabbas or Jesus who is called the Messiah?" For he realized that it was out of jealousy that they had handed Him over. While he was sitting on the judgment seat, his wife sent word to him, "Have nothing to do with that innocent man, for today I have suffered a great deal because of a dream about Him."

The Testimony of Claudia:

My name is Claudia Procula, granddaughter of the Emperor Augustus and wife of Marcus Pontius Pilatus, who was the Fifth Prefect of the Roman Province of Judaea, serving under Emperor Tiberius during the time of the prosecution and execution of the man named Jesus. By birth and position, I am a member of the Roman aristocracy, a member of the ruling class.

Although I had the typical education that young women of the aristocracy had, which by comparison to men, was minimal, I consider myself to be intellectually curious, mentally flexible, and morally adept. I try to be open to other ways of thinking and to both the traditional moral values of Roman culture and to those values of other cultures that I find interesting or meaningful. Pilate and I were married in Rome. I was twenty-three, and he was thirty-two. As the granddaughter of Augustus and the niece of Emperor Tiberius, I was a very desirable bride for any young man of ambition. Pilate was of a lesser noble family, and he had just returned from a successful campaign in Spain in which he accounted very well for himself as a Tribune in the battle for Toletum. His unit led the final charge against the fortifications of Toletum, breaking the ranks of the defenders, causing them to retreat and ultimately surrender. He was about to be promoted, but he was desirous of a life in politics and hungry for greater responsibility. Those were not the only reasons I married him, however. He was genuinely of strong moral character and had a sensitivity and concern in his treatment of others, though he showed an inclination to subordinate his principles to opportunities for success or promotion. I had genuine affection for him, and as we grew together, he learned to respect and to value my opinion.

Our union was a successful one. Within five years of marriage, he was appointed as the Fifth Prefect, or Pro-Consul, of the Roman Province of Judaea. This was not what one would call a plum assignment because of its distance from Rome, but it did mean Pilate would report directly to Rome and to Caesar. He became the governor, responsible for all military and civil decisions for a territory with a population of two million people. We were both overjoyed with this appointment, even though Judaea was not as desirable a location as many provinces in Germania, Hispania, or even Britannia. It had a history of being troublesome, and Rome had on-again, off-again troubles with the local population of Jews. If we could create a period of five to ten years of peace, during which there were no rebellious outbursts to get Rome's attention, this would be considered success.

Our military is respected and feared by the local population, and since it is accepted as a positive force in their midst, our tenure had all the potential to be very successful. We believed this was very doable, but not necessarily easy, because there was one very significant variable, albeit dormant, but still real. The Jews were compliant and cooperative in civil affairs but not at all in religious matters. They worshiped one God and one God only and would not tolerate any of their members participating in any event celebrating or worshipping Roman or other gods. We knew this was an issue on which there could be no compromise on the part of the Jews. We learned that lesson in the Maccabean Wars of insurrection 150 years ago and the mass suicide of Jews at Masada. However, in recent times, Tiberius made two decisions of genius to significantly defuse this problem. He appointed Herod the King of Israel, which gave the Jews some sense of independence similar to their past history; and he gave them autonomy in their religious beliefs and practices without interference from Rome. In return, the Jews promised to pay their taxes and not to be rebellious. Pilate and I thought that, with these decisions in place, we could not lose.

As I lived in Jerusalem, I developed relationships with many Jewish women, which afforded me the opportunity to learn about their religion, their beliefs, and their practices. As much as their belief in one God was a mystery to me, I learned it was a mystery that made sense to them, given the role their God played in their lives or that they believed He had played. Once I understood that, it was not difficult to understand their inflexibility in accepting belief in more than one god. I must admit that I too was favoring their beliefs. My friendships with these women ranged from those who were genuinely interesting, who enjoyed my company and who wanted nothing from me, to those who tolerated me more for the fact that I am Pilate's wife and could be of benefit to them or their husbands, to the servant girls who assisted me in maintaining our house. I found the servant girls to be among the most honest and the most loyal.

Our assignment in Judaea proceeded without issue for the first five years, and we knew we were on track for a return to Rome and a bigger/better assignment, with Pilate possibly being given an appointment to the Senate. The first inkling of a problem arose with the preacher and rabble-rouser John the Baptist. But this problem was religious in nature, and therefore of no importance to Pilate or Rome, as it was up to Herod and the religious authorities to handle. And handle it they did – in a very foolish, heavy-handed manner, one that created a martyr of the Baptist and fed the flames of rebellion, not so much against Rome as against Herod. If Herod can contain the rebellion, no harm is done; if he is unable to, then the rebellion has the potential to grow and impact Rome. Luckily for us, the zealots did not get their way, and things calmed down again for about three years.

The next time it was not a firebrand preacher like John the Baptist, but a quiet, humble, even meek preacher named Jesus. Two of the servants in my charge had heard Him preach and were witnesses to some of the healing of the sick and lame that He had done. When they spoke of him, calmness became visible in their faces, their bodies became serene, and a sense of peace exuded from them. It was remarkable to see. They explained He was just a simple man who preached God's love for everyone and that we needed to return that love to God by loving each other. They explained that he asked for nothing, wanted nothing, and preferred being with the poor and the sinful rather than the rich and powerful. They believed He was a prophet, a man blessed by God to do God's work. How else could He heal the lame and the sick and cast out demons? I never heard Jesus preach, but I must admit I was favorably disposed to Him and to His message.

It was the week before the celebration of the Jewish Passover, when there was a hint of something creating a public disturbance. I questioned the two women in my charge about the event I had heard about – that Jesus had returned to Jerusalem riding on a donkey and that there were crowds greeting Him as if He were a King returning

52

from a victorious battle. They confirmed that it was true, that there was a crowd, but that the crowd was merely acknowledging that he was a man of God and that was why they chanted, "Hosanna in the Highest." They explained that hosanna meant a shout of praise or adoration; an acclamation; and often used as an appeal to God for deliverance or in praise of God. I asked if that meant they were cheering Him because they accepted Him as a god, and they said emphatically no; they only cheered him as a representative of and from God. I do not know why, but something deep in me was creating discomfort. There was something happening here that I did not understand, a real sense of foreboding came over me, but I did not understand why.

As I went through my week in a semi-distracted state, my concern began to become more real when, on Thursday at about 7:00 at night, both of my Jewish servants came rushing to me as I was assembling flowers into an arrangement. They were very excited and very concerned. They told me things had changed drastically for Jesus, as Caiaphas had sent soldiers to arrest Him on charges of blasphemy. I asked what that meant, but they were not sure. They believed Jesus would be taken to the Sanhedrin for trial. My first thought was that this is good because it does not involve Roman law and therefore should not involve my husband. But my foreboding became stronger and more insistent. I told the two servants they were to take turns attending all the events involving Jesus after His arrest and to report back to me upon their return.

About midnight, they reported that Jesus was being tried by the Sanhedrin and they expected that to take a few hours. They explained things were moving fast because they had to be done before the Passover started less than twenty-four hours later. They did not know what the possible next step could be. I tried to sleep. My sleep was often disrupted by ugly, scary, and confusing images, none of which I could make any sense of. Finally, just before the servants told me their devastating news at about 8:00 AM on Friday, I had a brief period of real sleep in which my foreboding came to fruition, and I was clearly told in my dream what was happening and what should be done or not done to the man Jesus. The vision in my dream was very disturbing and confusing. At first, I was filled with dread, perspiration covered my body, and a depth of fear permeated my soul like I had never experienced. Slowly my dream became calmer, and a voice told me clearly that Jesus was a very special man and a very holy man; He was not a blasphemer and was not deserving of any punishment. As I awoke from this dream, still groggy, the servants entered in great excitement and told me the one piece of news I did not want to hear. They explained that the Sanhedrin had decided Jesus must die for His sin of blasphemy; but they did not have the authority to sentence a man to execution, so Jesus was referred to Pontius Pilate for trial because only Pilate could give a sentence of death.

My foreboding finally became clear. This was no longer a religious issue; it had become a political one and suddenly, my husband had become a prime decision-maker. If my husband sentenced Jesus to death, it would be his, no, our downfall; and events would unfold that we could not control. The trial was to begin in forty-five minutes, so it was impossible for me to dress and get there in time to speak with Pilate. The only other option was to send him a note telling him of my dream and of my belief that this man's life would be the key to our success or lack thereof. In my haste, I sent the note that read, "Have nothing to do with that innocent man, for today I have suffered a great deal because of a dream about Him." I wish I could have written more, gone into more detail regarding what I had seen in my dream, but there was no time... no time. I had to trust in my relationship with my husband. He had always respected and valued my opinion, but on those occasions, we spoke face to face. Could he, would he, see and understand the gravity of his decision to execute or not execute Jesus? I believed my husband loved me, but there was one thing that was a greater motivator for him than my love, and that was fear of disappointing Rome and Caesar. I was not hopeful that he would say no to the execution.

A few hours later, the servants returned and informed me that they were successful in getting the note to Pilate. They explained his strong reluctance to sentence Jesus to death because he could find no guilt in Him. He even tried to have the crowd select Jesus for pardon, but instead, they selected a known criminal, a murderer and revolutionary named Barabbas. The final straw seemed to be when the crowd implied that my husband would not be loyal to Rome if he did not sentence to death a man who claimed to be king, since there was only one king and that was Caesar. I knew that Pilate could never tolerate such an accusation, so I was not at all surprised that Pilate finally consented to the crucifixion of Jesus. I left the two servants, returned to my room, and sobbed uncontrollably. I cried for the death of an innocent man, and I cried to calm the pain in my breast because I knew the death of this man would be a problem for Rome and ultimately would destroy my husband's promising career.

Chapter 7
The Seventh Witness – Decimus

Pilate has Jesus Flogged (Luke 23:3-16)

Pilate then called together the chief priests, the leaders, and the people, and said to them, "You brought me this man as one who was perverting the people; and here I have examined Him in your presence and have not found this man guilty of any of your charges against Him. Neither has Herod, for He sent Him back to us. Indeed, He has done nothing to deserve death. I will therefore have Him flogged and release Him."

The Crowd Screams for Jesus' Crucifixion (Matt 27:20-23)

Now the chief priests and the elders persuaded the crowds to ask for Barabbas and to have Jesus killed. The governor again said to them, "Which of the two do you want me to release for you?" And they said, "Barabbas." Pilate said to them, "Then what should I do with Jesus who is called the Messiah?" All of them said, "Let Him be crucified!" Then he asked, "Why, what evil has He done?" But they shouted all the more, "Let Him be crucified!"

The Testimony of Decimus:

My name is Decimus. My name is appropriate as I am the tenth child of my father, who had three wives. I was born in Gaul and was conscripted into the Roman Army at age 17 after our tribe was defeated by the Romans. I have been a soldier for twelve years and was recently promoted to the rank of Decanus, a commander of a ten-man unit or squad. I belong to the XI Tribune of the XVI Cohort of the III Legion, assigned to Palestine and North Africa. I was assigned the additional duty of flogging prisoners fourteen months ago, and, I must admit, it is not a duty I particularly like. However, the first obligation of a Roman soldier is to obey orders, and any indication given that you are unable or unwilling to execute those orders to the very best of your ability will result in reassignment to a frontline duty (at best) or being tried and punished for dereliction of duty. When I was assigned this duty, I learned very quickly that, to succeed in the Roman Army, I must become the best flogger my commander has ever seen.

Since I have had this duty, I have made it my habit to not know anything about the prisoner to be flogged. All I need to know are when to do the flogging and how many lashes are to be administered. With this mindset, I have flogged dozens of prisoners, some of them fellow soldiers; and I was always able to keep a professional distance so that nothing, not sympathy, not compassion, not personal concern, not justice, would affect the delivery of my lashes. I use a whip called a flagrum. The flagrum is a whip with a short handle and generally two or three long, thick thongs, each weighted at some distance from their extremity with lead balls or mutton bones. In action, the thongs cut the skin, while the balls or bones create deep contusions. The result is significant hemorrhaging and considerable weakening of the vital resistance of the victim. Before a crucifixion, the benefit of such a flogging, if one may call it that, is that it shortens the agony of the prisoner on the cross.

I do not remember specific floggings except in unique or special cases, but I do remember the flogging of the man Jesus. I remember it because He was different, and His situation was different. For one thing, I usually only flog criminals, persons convicted of a crime against Rome and sentenced to be crucified. Jesus was a Jew and a self-proclaimed man of God—the Jewish God—who, by all reports, was a preacher who went from town-to-town preaching of His God's mercy. He also performed many signs in healing the sick and the possessed. He did not seem to be much of a criminal. When he was brought to me, the Pro-Consul, Pilate, had said He was not guilty of any crime, but to placate the crowd, He would have Him flogged and then sent away. Apparently, the crowd would have none of that and kept demanding He be crucified; and Pilate finally gave into their demands, allegedly because He was afraid of them rioting in the streets.

I take no pleasure in flogging innocent men; but I am a soldier, and above all else, I obey orders. When he was brought to me, He had already been beaten. His tunic was blood-stained and dried, and fresh blood streaked on His face; bruises were obvious where He had been hit by fists or other objects. We removed His tunic and ensured He was secured in a loin cloth. He was bent forward over a rounded stone with his hands and arms extended at full length, 45 degrees from His body. His hands were tied to prevent movement of His torso, and His feet were shackled to rings in the ground. Being right-handed, I stood behind Him about three feet away and to the left of His left shoulder, so that my blows would be delivered diagonally across His back. It is Roman law that floggings in preparation for crucifixion be limited to 39 blows, so that the prisoner would have enough strength to carry His cross to the place of execution.

Normally, when I deliver the first strike of the flagrum, the prisoner cries out loudly in an explosion of breath to expel the rush of pain that He experiences, but this man did not do so. Neither did He do so on the second, or the tenth, or the twentieth, or any of the others that followed. I was surprised, no, intrigued, as this was way beyond normal. I have flogged bigger men, tougher men, meaner men, and very nasty men, and they all cried out in anguish; most begged for me to stop before I reached 20. Yet this man, of no imposing stature, uttered not a word. Whatever was happening, I was somehow involved. It was not normal. I knew normal, I experienced normal most days of my life, and this was not normal. No human being made of flesh and blood is capable of such strength. No human being is capable of rejecting such pain and suppressing the normal response of vocal cries to alleviate its intensity.

For the first time that I can recall, I started to struggle in doing my job. I could not get over the fact that a man, who from all reports I had heard was a preacher and a healer but who angered His Jewish leaders, could deserve such treatment, which was worse than what the most criminal of criminals received. As I approached the maximum of 39 blows, I tried to reduce the force of those remaining blows. There was hardly any undamaged skin left on His back. If He were to receive treatment immediately, it would take Him weeks to fully recover. I wanted this to stop, but as I have told you, I am a soldier and I obey orders. One of my assistants noticed He was close to passing out, and I felt great relief when I finally delivered the 39th blow. I went to assist in releasing His restraints and our eyes met. His eyes were amazingly soft, not from pain, but, I thought, from compassion. How could this man that I had beaten near to the point of death have compassion for me? This was more than I could bear. Tears came to my eyes, so I quickly hid my face from the others in order that I would not be accused of being weak. Why did He not hate me or beg for mercy like all the others I had flogged? Many of those who could talk would curse me, yet He said nothing.

There was concern that He was too weak and would not be able to carry His cross. We were told to give Him some water and He would carry His cross when the time came. No longer surprised at what this man could do, I saw that, when the time came, He carried his cross. I do not know how many I have killed in my life as a soldier. Certainly, many on the battlefield; some who were civilians protesting against Rome; and many others who were condemned to death after a legal trial. I have never had regret over what I have done as a soldier in service to Rome, until now. I participated in this man's death; I played a very major role, and I am not at all proud of that. For the first time as a soldier of Rome, I felt… believed… that I did something wrong in following my orders. The memory of these events stayed with me for a very long time, often disturbing my sleep, forcing me to wake up, sometimes in a state of panic and often soaked with perspiration. I was desperate for this torment to stop because sooner or later my colleagues would hear my distress and my effectiveness as a soldier would be questioned, my career destroyed. I decided the only option open to me was to find out more about this man Jesus. Once I made that decision and started my search for answers about Jesus, my night terrors diminished, and my anxiety came under control. I heard the preaching of James and Matthew, after which I knew I was on the right path. But I also had this quiet foreboding, that I would have to make more personal decisions that would change my life forever.

Chapter 8
The Eighth Witness – Judas Iscariot

The Soldiers Mock Jesus and Pilate hands him over to be Crucified (John 19:2-12)

And the soldiers wove a crown of thorns and put it on His head, and they dressed Him in a purple robe. They kept coming up to Him, saying, "Hail, King of the Jews!" and striking Him on the face. Pilate went out again and said to them, "Look, I am bringing Him out to you to let you know that I find no case against him." So, Jesus came out, wearing the crown of thorns and the purple robe. Pilate said to them, "Here is the man!" When the chief priests and the police saw Him, they shouted, "Crucify Him! Crucify Him!" Pilate said to them, "Take Him yourselves and crucify Him; I find no case against Him." The Jews answered him, "We have a law, and according to that law, He ought to die because He has claimed to be the Son of God." Now when Pilate heard this, he was more afraid than ever. He entered his headquarters again and asked Jesus, "Where are you from?" But Jesus gave him no answer. Pilate therefore said to Him, "Do you refuse to speak to me? Do you not know that I have power to release you, and power to crucify you?" Jesus answered him, "You would have no power over Me unless it had been given you from above; therefore, the one who handed Me over to you is guilty of a greater sin." From then on Pilate tried to release Him, but the Jews cried out, "If you release this man, you are no friend of the emperor. Everyone who claims to be a king sets himself against the emperor."

The Suicide of Judas (Matt 27:3-10)

When Judas, His betrayer, saw that Jesus was condemned, he repented and brought back the thirty pieces of silver to the chief priests and the elders. He said, "I have sinned by betraying innocent blood." But they said, "What is that to us? See to it yourself." Throwing down the pieces of silver in the temple, he departed; and he went and hanged Himself. But the chief priests, taking the pieces of silver, said, "It is not lawful to put them into the treasury, since they are blood money." After conferring together, they used them to buy the potter's field as a place to bury foreigners. For this reason, that field has been called the Field of Blood to this day. Then was fulfilled what had been spoken through the prophet Jeremiah, "And they took the thirty pieces of silver, the price of the one on whom a price had been set, on whom some of the people of Israel had set a price, and they gave them for the potter's field, as the Lord commanded me."

The Testimony of Judas:

My name is Judas Iscariot, and I am a disciple of Jesus the Christ. Before I met Jesus, I was an overachiever and was able to take advantage of opportunities so that eventually I gained a basic education and learned how to handle money. I am a Jew, born in Nain, just south of Nazareth and north of the Samarian border. My father is a merchant, and he taught me well, not just about money but also about the prophecy that God will send us a Messiah to return all Israel to its former glory.

I am one of the original twelve, and for three years, I spent virtually every day in the presence of Jesus and had the key responsibility of managing the group's money. I protected our money; I created and managed the budget; I made sure we had food to eat and wine to drink. I did not consider it a sin to pay myself for all the services I did; to me, it was a normal business expense. I was present at His healings and at His preaching. I was present when He fed five thousand people with five loaves of bread and two fish. When Jesus commanded us to go two by two to preach His message and gave us the power to cast out demons and heal the sick, I went with Nathaniel to the South and did as we were commanded. I was present when He cried over the death of His friend Lazarus, and I was present when He became very angry at the tradespeople in the temple whom He believed corrupted His father's house.

He was a difficult man to read; sometimes He was simple, wanting nothing, asking for nothing, yet giving all. Sometimes He was a very complex person, who taught in parables; who spoke of faith and of love in a manner that we did not understand; and who obviously had a connection with God that David and the prophets did not have. He was an innocent man, a man who lived a life as close to perfection as I could imagine. He was humble, totally without desire for anything for Himself, and who disdained having things and physical comfort because they were distractions to His purpose, which was to reveal the Kingdom of God to all who would listen. He was complex sometimes in His preaching or in His arguments or in His answers to questions when He did not make a clear and direct statement or give a clear and direct answer. Instead, He spoke in riddles, sometimes leaving you with opposing thoughts, or very foggy, unclear answers that had you asking yourself, "What does He mean?" I later found out He did this on purpose so that, in time, when you did get to the clarity of His answer, the answer would be more meaningful and more comprehensive than if He just told you the first time.

As I spent more time with Him, I truly came to believe that He was the Messiah, the one sent by God to save the people of Israel from their enemies, the one who would be greater than David and return the Kingdom of Israel to something greater than it was before, a kingdom that would live without fear of any enemy. I completely agreed with His message of love, but I was confused by His vision, or lack thereof, and His willingness to accept the status quo of Israel's position in the world in His vision of the kingdom of God. I saw His power; and I believed He had power He never showed us. I believed, no, I knew, He had the power to summon the angels of heaven to be His agents—his soldiers, if need be—to return Israel to its former glory and to free us from the domination of Rome. Didn't His father personally support Moses and use his awesome power to protect his people and to destroy the Egyptians? Didn't His father directly intercede with Joshua, enabling the Israelites to defeat the overwhelming forces of the Canaanites and Moabites as they secured the promised land? And did he not enable the Judges to protect his people from the more powerful Philistines, Midianites, and other enemies in Canaan? Certainly, the Judges could not be more powerful than Jesus, the elect of God.

Since God had done all these things and since I knew He was the Messiah, God's messenger, God's angel of action, who would deliver his people from domination by a perverse and heathen empire, how did He not know it? If I knew He was the new Moses who would save the people of God, not by escaping slavery from an idolatrous nation but by vanquishing the enemies of Israel and making Israel once again the greatest power on earth, why did he not know it? Did God not tell Abraham:

"And I will give to you, and to your offspring after you, the land where you are now an alien, all the land of Canaan, for a perpetual holding; and I will be their God." (Gen 17:8)

Was this prophecy of Israel's dominance in the land of Canaan not the same as the Kingdom of God to come that He preached? And did God not promise David that his Kingdom would last forever? How can this be the kingdom David created when we are ruled by idolaters? Are we not the offspring of Abraham, and are we not supposed to be the rulers of the land of Canaan forever?

By the conclusion of the second year of my time with Him, my frustration with His lack of action and His lack of stated intent to change the status quo grew, and I concluded that what He intended to do was not what I believed needed to be done. I still held open the possibility that He would do what I, and so many others, saw as the obvious solution – rebellion against and conquering Rome. But that time never seemed to come. I began to understand that His message of peace was all-encompassing, that he would never tolerate violence for any purpose, and that he most certainly would never initiate violence, not even for the rebirth of Israel. This disconnect between my belief and his teaching began to weigh on me; and I knew I could not afford to keep drifting along in the hope that something would happen for Him to become the man, the king, I knew He was intended to be.

I then told myself I just had to be patient and to wait for the time when it was right for Him to strike. And then, with our return to Jerusalem for the Passover, I saw an opportunity. It was then that I decided I had to push events in a way that would yield the result I envisioned. If Jesus would not initiate war against Rome, then maybe I could have Rome initiate war against Jesus, and He would be forced to not just defend Himself but in effect, all of Israel, because Rome would not punish just Him but all the Jewish people.

It was then that I met with the High priests and members of the Sanhedrin and agreed to deliver Jesus to them. They surprised me by asking what I wanted, then quickly said they would give me 30 pieces of silver. At first, I was highly insulted and offended. Money? Betray a human being, especially a friend, for money? This is not about money! This is about the future of Israel! Just as quickly, I realized I had to restrain my indignation, because corrupt people only understand corrupt motives in the people they deal with, and for better or worse, they were dealing with me. I had to have a corrupt motive for them to accept that I was exactly who I was presenting myself to be – a corrupt and despicable person who is willing to sell a friend's life for a few denarii. If I had explained my true motives, they would have rejected me, and very probably arrested me. So, filled with disgust, and in order to start the process that would result in the resurrection of Israel, I willingly said yes, 30 pieces of silver would do.

I believe I was the only one of the disciples to fully understand that Jesus was going to His death in Jerusalem. He gave us many hints that His mission required Him to die and to rise again; the others just chose to not hear or to believe that. He told us when we were in Bethany and Mary anointed His head with expensive perfume and I complained that it was a waste of money; He reprimanded me, saying that what she had done was in preparation for His burial. The others chose to ignore that, but I did not. If He were so willing to go to His death, it would be beneficial to all Israel if His arrest and prosecution could result in Israel escaping the domination of Rome. The plan was to have Him arrested, brought before the Sanhedrin, then Pilate, to be ridiculed and condemned as an artificial prophet, one who came from Satan and not from God, and finally that He was an enemy of Rome. This, I believed, was all that it would take for Him to call upon His Father to have this most grievous mistake corrected; and the correction would be made with the sword, directed by God, and implemented by His angels, just as he had done to Sodom and Gomorrah. Under no conditions could He die. Why would he die? For what reason? He is God's agent, his personal messenger, the one given the responsibility to bring Israel into unity with God by accepting and living his message of love. No, under no conditions would he die. I must have faith that He would complete His divine mission.

After watching His trial and seeing that He made no response and offered no defense, it became clear that He would not fight; that there would be no request to His Father to send a legion of angels to chastise the sinners, the idolaters, and the oppressors of Israel. At first, I was just confused as to how my thinking could have been so wrong. Then Pilate made his final decision, and I became agitated and then insanely angry. I did not want Him to die – that was not the plan! In a much-heightened state of anxiety, I ran to Caiaphas and other priests in the Sanhedrin and told them that this must stop, that Jesus must not be executed, that He was innocent. They were not moved by my protestations and sent me away; after all, I was the one who betrayed Him in the first place.

After that, my memory is less clear; but I recall the terrible feeling in my stomach, the total state of panic I was in, as I tried to think of some way to stop the execution. But there was none. I remember throwing the 30 pieces of silver at Caiaphas and his Sanhedrin colleagues and running from them as fast as I could, with no place to run to. Thoughts flooded my mind, fleeting thoughts, confusing thoughts, self-incriminating thoughts. How is it He is to be crucified? Executed like a common criminal? Where are you, God? Was He your son or not? Do you not care what will happen to Him? Do you not care that, if He is killed, He would not complete his mission? My confusion raged, as I asked myself a myriad of questions and received no reply.

In my panic, the reality of what I had done became very clear. It is I who crucified Him! It is I who scourged Him! It is I who drove the nails in His hands and his feet! It is I who pierced His side with the spear! Certainly, there was no villain on earth worse than I.

I stopped somewhere and felt this overpowering darkness come upon me. Self-incriminating thoughts demanding answers as to how I could have been so foolish, so wrong, flooded my mind. These thoughts and the darkness enveloping me were like an oppressive weight bearing down on me. I could not get away from it, nor could I lessen the pressure it put upon me and the pain that was emanating from every molecule in my body. The darkness came upon me in waves, each one more powerful than the one before. I struggled; I tried to fight it, but the pain and fear became more overwhelmingly oppressive. I tried to scream but no sound came from my throat. The darkness became darker still with a beckoning force that seemingly offered rest and promised peace I could not resist. Being in the darkness was like swirling in a vortex and falling in a bottomless pit. I spread my arms hoping to latch onto a lifeline but there was none. I was scared, confused, and incapable of rational thought. I became so very weary that I just wanted to rest...I needed rest...finally, lost in a whirlpool of nothingness and spent of all energy, I welcomed the darkness and surrendered to it.

Chapter 9
The Ninth Witness – Veronica

Luke 23: 27-31

A great number of the people followed Him, and among them were women who were beating their breasts and wailing for Him. But Jesus turned to them and said, "Daughters of Jerusalem, do not weep for Me, but weep for yourselves and for your children. For the days are surely coming when they will say, 'Blessed are the barren, and the wombs that never bore, and the breasts that never nursed.' Then they will begin to say to the mountains, 'Fall on us'; and to the hills, 'Cover us.' For if they do this when the wood is green, what will happen when it is dry?"

Veronica Wipes the Face of Jesus [From the Narrative of the Sixth Station of the Stations of the Cross Devotion]

According to Catholic Church tradition, Veronica was moved with sympathy when she saw Jesus carrying His cross to Golgotha and gave Him her veil that He might wipe his forehead. Jesus accepted the offering, held it to his face, and then handed it back to Her—the image of His face miraculously impressed upon it. This piece of cloth became known as the Veil of Veronica. The quote from the Devotion reads: "Suddenly, a woman comes out of the crowd. Her name is Veronica. You can see how she cares for you as she takes a cloth and begins to wipe the blood and sweat from your face. She can't do much, but she offers what little help she can."

The Testimony of Veronica:

My name is Veronica. I am a Jewess, and a native of Jerusalem. I met Mary, Joseph, and Jesus when they came to Jerusalem for Passover many years ago when Jesus was a child, and over the years I got to know them fairly well, although we did not see each other very often. I remember when Jesus was a boy, and Mary and Joseph could not find Him among their relatives when they were returning to Nazareth from Jerusalem. I was one of the first persons they came to see in Jerusalem if, by some mistake or miracle, that Jesus was with me, because they had spent time at my house. Mary was so worried that when I told her I had not seen Jesus, I thought she was going to faint. Joseph was stalwart, however, and he laid out a plan to check with everyone they knew in Jerusalem. Mary agreed and said she would go to the temple to rest and pray. Of course, it was there that she found Jesus engaged in discussion with the priests and scribes.

It was not very difficult to see and to understand that Jesus was not just another boy. Although He behaved very much like the boys His age, He was different. He had qualities not readily found in young boys or young men. Most particularly, I noticed He was very considerate of Mary, never giving her cause to worry or to be concerned about His safety. I think He learned a valuable lesson from that independent excursion He made when He was twelve years old. He also exuded serenity, a natural inclination for solitude and prayer, and a generosity of spirit unlike anything I have seen in a young person. Jesus loved Joseph and worked with him for many years. He became a very competent carpenter, working the business effectively after Joseph's death until he began His ministry of teaching and preaching.

The last time I saw Jesus was when I attended the marriage feast of a young couple in Cana. I did not personally witness the miraculous change of water into wine that was the talk of the event, but I personally spoke with the Chief Steward and the servants, and each one confirmed that Jesus had changed the water into wine. This was no charlatan's trick as I and dozens of guests enjoyed this new wine. I did not know exactly what to think, but it confirmed to me the special relationship I had observed that Jesus had with God. I had not seen Him after that until His triumphant arrival in Jerusalem, but of course, I heard of His work, his preaching, and the many signs He had worked. It was interesting that when people spoke about Him, they always spoke first about His words, what He said, not the signs He worked, not what He did. His fame rose considerably when He taught many, many people that they were special to God, blessed by God, and that they would be united with Him in heaven.

"Blessed are the poor in spirit," He said, "for theirs is the kingdom of heaven."

He was talking about us, about me, my family, and my neighbors. We are the poor in spirit, the humble who love God, live by His rules, and work ceaselessly to be a part of His Kingdom. And Jesus tells us we are successful, and that we will attain the kingdom of heaven. For us, these words were more valuable than manna from heaven. When I heard, He was coming to Jerusalem for Passover and that many people wanted to greet Him as He entered the city, I had to join them. I saw Him on that donkey's colt, and I was one of those throwing palm leaves in front of Him and shouting:

"Hosanna, blessed is He who comes in the name of the Lord." (Matt 21:9)

I went to see Mary on Tuesday before Passover to catch up on all that we had missed since we last saw each other. Although we had a very good visit, there was a distraction about her, a sense of fear, possibly, or at least of concern. I asked her if something was wrong, and she could only say she was not sure. She invited me to the Passover meal that she would celebrate with Jesus and His followers, but I was unable to go.

I heard nothing more until Friday, about 9:00 in the morning. My relative Serena, who knew of my relationship to, and love of, Mary and Jesus, came to my home and told me of Jesus' approaching trial at the Praetorium, and that the Sanhedrin and the High Priest Caiaphas were pushing very hard for His execution. I was shocked and immediately thought of my friend Mary, but given the hour and the day, there was no way I could get to her before the trial started, and once it began, I would never find her. I did not know what to do but wait. Wait to hear the verdict; wait to hear the sentence; wait to see if some miracle would happen. The trial with Pilate was relatively short, and as I later found out, the verdict was no surprise. Typical of Roman practice, the verdict would be carried out immediately, and since Passover began at sunset, the execution must be completed by the ninth hour in the middle of the afternoon. Heartbroken, I decided the only thing I could do was to go to a place on the Road of Sorrows and wait to see Jesus pass by. I am not sure why I wanted to do this; I think I believed in some way I could help.

My cousin Serena, I, and a few other friends went to the Road of Sorrows and found the place I had in mind and waited. Our wait was not long. Just before the 6th hour (midday), we saw the approaching column of soldiers and three prisoners carrying their crosses. Jesus was the last of the three, and he was followed by soldiers, then members of the Sanhedrin. As the others passed and Jesus approached me, the words of the Prophet Isaiah rang loud and clear in my mind:

"He had no form or comeliness that we should look at Him, and no beauty that we should desire Him. He was despised and rejected by men; a man of sorrows and acquainted with grief; and as one from whom men hide their faces. He was despised, and we esteemed Him not." (Isaiah 52:2-3)

I shuddered at the sight; at what they had done to Him. It seemed my very heart was in tears. As He approached, He shouldered His cross at the joint of the vertical and horizontal pieces, the end of the vertical piece dragging on the ground, making a scraping sound as it moved, then a thud as it dropped some inches due to cobblestones and the uneven road. The procession stopped, and Jesus was directly in front of me, about eight feet away. He looked directly at me, and that compassionate look I had seen before from the boy and the young man was on His face and made my knees buckle. His face was dirty with stains of dried blood, and perspiration ran down His face. I could not restrain myself, and I have no memory of what I did. I apparently walked up to Him, tears streaming down my face, and wiped His face with a soft cloth that I had with me. I was so filled with sorrow and pain that I said nothing, nor did He. But I am certain He remembered me; I am certain he accepted my love; and I am certain he wanted to comfort me as much as I wanted to comfort Him.

Our interaction only lasted a moment, as the guards pushed me away and started yelling about moving forward. I could not follow the procession. I stayed at that place with my friends for a long time before having the strength to walk home. It was not until the next day, as I was straightening up, that I noticed He had left a perfect impression of His face on the cloth I used to wipe His face. His final gift to one who loved Him, which He returned as an acknowledgment of a kindness rendered to Him. I needed to share this with Mary, to tell her how her son gave me a blessing that I did not have words to fully explain, and that this blessing bonded me to Him forever.

Chapter 10
The Tenth Witness – Simon of Cyrene

Jesus Carries His Cross (Mark 15:21-24)

They compelled a passer-by, who was coming in from the country, to carry His cross; it was Simon of Cyrene, the father of Alexander and Rufus. Then they brought Jesus to the place called Golgotha (which means the place of a skull). And they offered Him wine mixed with myrrh; but He did not take it. And they crucified Him, and divided His clothes among them, casting lots to decide what each should take.

The Testimony of Simon of Cyrene:

My name is Simon, and I am from Cyrene. Cyrene is located on the North African coast in northeastern Libya. I am a camel trader by profession, having worked in this trade since I was thirteen years old. A lifetime of hard work feeding, raising, training, and trading camels caused me to grow tall and to develop a strong body, particularly in my arms, shoulders, and back. I am a Jewish convert. My wife is a Jewess who was born and raised in Cyrene due to an earlier exile of her ancestors who were taken from Israel and resettled in Cyrene.

I come to Jerusalem from time to time on business, but this trip was special as I brought my two boys, Alexander and Rufus, to worship in the temple and celebrate Passover in Jerusalem for the first time in their lives. I was on my way to complete our Passover preparations when I came across a procession of soldiers escorting three prisoners to the place of crucifixion. A crowd of people stood on the sidewalk watching them pass by, so I stopped also to let them pass. As the soldiers passed, one of the prisoners fell with the horizontal arm of His cross laying on top of His shoulders. The Centurion in charge of the procession looked around and saw me, probably because I stood a head above all others, called me over, and told me to help the fellow who had fallen carry His cross.

"Why me?" I protested. "I am a visitor; I have nothing to do with your prisoner or your execution." The Centurion was unmoved by my protestations and, in a very unpleasant voice, ordered me to pick up the cross. I have been around Romans long enough to know you do not disobey the orders of a Roman Centurion.

Not wanting any trouble, I stooped down and used my legs to lift the cross. It was very heavy. I marveled at the prisoner, whose clothes on His back were covered in blood, which told me He had been savagely beaten, and wondered how He could have carried these roughly hewn logs in the first place. As I lifted the log from His back, I later found out he presented Himself as some sort of Messiah, turned His head towards me, and our eyes met. Something strange happened. His eyes were soft; to me, they seemed to be more filled with compassion and gratitude than with pain or anger. It was as if He was thanking me for my help.

Then I felt a subtle but real infusion of energy in my body, one that enabled me to lift the log more easily and secure it on my shoulders. He struggled to get up, finally making it to one knee, and one of the guards in frustration pulled Him to his feet because He was too slow in getting up to walk. As He took His first step free of the load He had carried, He looked at me again, and this time I saw gratitude, and again felt a surge of energy from His gaze, enabling me to start walking, carrying His load but not feeling any great strain in doing so.

I found out later that when the Centurion asked me to carry His cross, that was the third time He had fallen, so the guards believed that

He did not have the strength to carry His cross to Golgotha – the place of execution. They were right. Luckily for me, Golgotha was no more than one-quarter mille pasuum (modern mile) away, and unluckily for me, it was uphill. Given the procession, the state of health of the prisoners, and the uphill walk, it took about twenty minutes for us to get to the top.

During the walk, I stared intently at the back of the one I was helping. I later found out his name was Jesus. He was obviously in pain; His back was bloodied, and he Had a most odious and ugly instrument of torture on His head. A vine with long thorns was woven in a circle to fit over his forehead and the back of His head. The thorns were long, a little more than one uncia (modern inch), and in the front where I could see them clearly, they were embedded in His forehead, causing blood to drip down his cheek. I wanted to wash His face and to somehow relieve His pain, but such a service was beyond me. He walked somewhat erratically in His gait but never lost his balance. We reached the summit, and the guards showed me where to lay His cross. I did as I was told and stood up, and saw Him directly in front of me, standing as erectly as He could, as one of the guards was taking His cloak off His shoulders.

In this last interaction with Him, our eyes met and locked onto each other. In His eyes, I saw gratitude; I saw compassion; I saw forgiveness; I saw a man at peace. I nodded my head slightly in acknowledgment of our unspoken communication. The guards completed disrobing Him, then, as they placed Him in the position of crucifixion on the cross, I turned my head. I did not wish to see what I knew would happen next. I started walking away, back down the hill and had not gotten very far when I heard the first strike of the heavily weighted hammer on the spikes being driven through His extremities to secure Him to the cross. I heard the heavy thud of the hammer striking the spike, but I did not hear a responding cry of pain. I kept walking. I did not look back. I did not want anyone to see the tears in my eyes.

Chapter 11
The Eleventh Witness – Dismas

The Crucifixion of Jesus (John 19:18)

So, they took Jesus; and carrying the cross by Himself, He went out to what is called The Place of the Skull, which in Hebrew is called Golgotha. There they crucified Him, and with Him two others, one on either side, with Jesus between them.

(Luke 23:39-42)

One of the criminals who were hanged there kept deriding Him and saying, "Are you not the Messiah? Save yourself and us!" But the other rebuked him, saying, "Do you not fear God, since you are under the same sentence of condemnation? And we indeed have been condemned justly, for we are getting what we deserve for our deeds, but this man has done nothing wrong." Then he said, "Jesus, remember me when you come into your kingdom." He replied, "Truly I tell you, today you will be with me in Paradise."

The Testimony of Dismas:

My name is Dismas. I am a Samaritan, 37 years old, and I am a thief. I, as are all Samaritans, am treated as an outcast by Jews because our ancestors intermarried with Assyrians after the conquest of the Northern Kingdom of Israel 500 years ago and mixed our worship of God with the worship of the Assyrian gods. This polluted the beliefs and ritual practices of Judaism and the teachings of the Law, so the

Jews of Israel and Judea consider us heretics and since then consider us to be unclean and therefore can have no contact with them. The Jews of Judaea believed this union between Assyrians and the Jews of Samaria to be worse than unacceptable because it polluted both the purity of Jewish blood and the purity of Judaism as they believed it to be.

I was born in Shechem, just south of Nablus, and moved to Judaea where the practice of my trade was more lucrative. My trade is thievery and all things illegal. I steal from the rich so that I can be rich; but no matter how much I steal, I never seem to get rich. The Jews of Judaea are a hateful people as they treat all Samaritans with disdain, which is why it gives me so much pleasure to steal from them. Although I try very hard to avoid violence, in my trade one must be prepared to defend himself, which I have done on occasion. The last time I defended myself, the result was one dead Roman soldier and another very badly wounded. That is why I was sentenced to death by crucifixion.

My memory of my crucifixion is very clear and very complete. I can only assume that when you are experiencing the most intolerable pain possible and you know you are about to die, the urge to live is so great that you latch onto every moment in some superstitious belief that somehow the inevitable will be held at bay. Of course, it never is, but the effort to stay alive in some magical way imprints all the events and words and actions of those last hours indelibly in your brain. At least that is the only explanation I have for why I am so sure of everything that I am about to tell you.

I had watched the prisoner Jesus when we were in the Praetorium. I saw that He received more lashes than Gestas and I. I saw that He was mocked and beaten; and I saw that awful vine with thorns placed on His head, causing me to realize that whatever pain I suffered, His was much worse. I first thought He must have done some really awful things to be treated so badly, so I asked one of the guards what He had done. I was shocked and in a state of total unbelief when the guard said He was a preacher, who healed people and told Caiaphas He was the Son of God. I was confused, and stupidly I continued to ask: Had He killed? No. Had He robbed? No. Had He raped? No. Had He kidnapped? No. Then why was He being executed? Politics. For some reason, this made me angry. The injustice was too despicable, even for one like me.

I continued watching Him and noticed how even, how balanced He was, even while in excruciating pain. There was no drama to Him. No weeping; no begging for medical care or for water or for food; just a seemingly quiet acceptance of His situation. I found this impressive because I would have been livid. I could not understand how He could have gotten a death sentence, and even more why He was not objecting strenuously to the injustice being done to Him.

My entire body was racked with pain as we hung on the cross. In my torment, I wished for a quick death when I heard His words to His father asking for forgiveness of those who had crucified Him. How could He think of others when He was in such insufferable pain? The sincerity in His voice was clear to me, and even in my pain, I was amazed that a human being could be capable of such love, of such forgiveness. Without knowing it, my focus changed from myself and my pain to this man, hanging on a cross a few feet away from me. I wanted to talk to Him, to ask Him if I could qualify for His father's forgiveness, but the words would not come. I became oblivious to my pain as my gaze focused on Him with an intensity that I cannot explain.

I do not know how many minutes passed, it seemed like an eternity, when I heard Gestas, the third of us to be crucified, speak to Jesus in a derisive and mocking tone, telling Him if he is the Son of God to save Himself and us also. When I heard Gestas, something snapped in me, and I had to respond to his insulting accusation.

I cannot say I was a good man in life. I could not count my victims or my sins if I tried. If I had a redeeming feature, it was that I never lied. I may steal and kill, but I never lie. For me, to not take responsibility for something you did was a lie, therefore I not only took responsibility for my actions, but I also often boasted about them. It just seemed to me that when you make a choice to do something, and you do it, you should accept the fact that you did it and not try to blame someone else for what you chose to do. That was what got me so upset with Gestas. Like me, Gestas was a criminal, and like me, he had killed others during or after his crimes. Unlike me, he did not kill to defend himself or to stop armed soldiers from arresting him; he had killed innocent, unarmed people he had robbed. This is why I could not stand his hypocrisy, and because I could not stand it, I could not ignore it.

I had no intention of currying favor with the man Jesus. Without thinking it, I responded to Gestas in as loud a voice as I could muster, reprimanding him for his question and reminding him that our punishment was just, but this man had done nothing. My response to Gestas was both from anger and my sense of what was decent, although it might seem incongruous that a thief such as I could have a sense of decency. I did not know in my mind or in my understanding that Jesus was indeed the Son of God; I did not know He could give me forgiveness and guarantee a place in heaven for me. But I knew He was not just different but special, I knew He was innocent, and I believed, based on the way He had handled himself, that He was favored by God, so my request to be remembered when He came into His kingdom was the only way I could think of to ask for forgiveness.

Even though He was in agony, the words of His response were clear and exactly what I wanted to hear; they were reaffirming and reassuring, and I immediately felt relief from the pain and the stress of my situation. But surprisingly, it was not the words that gave me the most relief; it was His tone of voice, the calmness of His demeanor, the love in His voice. I cannot adequately express to you what I felt and what I experienced after hearing those words, "Today you will be with me in Paradise" spoken with such love. Waves of calm came over me, the fear and stress that had tormented me since my arrest and that had increased to incalculable levels as I awaited death completely left me, and the horrific pain from hanging on the cross was no longer present. I felt renewed, like I had been given a new life. I believed I died with a smile on my face.

Chapter 12
The Twelfth Witness – Hannah

The Crucifixion of Jesus Continued (John 19:17-27)

Pilate also had an inscription written and put on the cross. It read, "Jesus of Nazareth, the King of the Jews." Many of the Jews read this inscription because the place where Jesus was crucified was near the city; and it was written in Hebrew, in Latin, and in Greek. Then the chief priests of the Jews said to Pilate, "Do not write, 'The King of the Jews,' but 'This man said, I am King of the Jews.'" Pilate answered, "What I have written I have written."

When the soldiers had crucified Jesus, they took His clothes and divided them into four parts, one for each soldier. They also took His tunic; now the tunic was seamless, woven in one piece from the top. So, they said to one another, "Let us not tear it, but cast lots for it to see who will get it." This was to fulfill what the scripture says: *"They divided my clothes among themselves, and for my clothing they cast lots."* (Ps 22:18) And that is what the soldiers did.

Meanwhile, standing near the cross of Jesus were His mother, and His mother's sister, Mary the wife of Clopas, and Mary Magdalene. When Jesus saw His mother and the disciple whom He loved standing beside her, He said to his mother, "Woman, here is your son." Then He said to the disciple, "Here is your mother." And from that hour, the disciple took her into His own home.

The Testimony of Hannah:

My name is Hannah. I am a Jewess from the province of Galilee. Mary and I live in Nazareth, and we have been friends since she first returned from Egypt with Joseph and Jesus, who was just a toddler then. We have shared meals together; we have prayed together in the temple; we have spent countless hours sewing clothes and talking about all that was happening in our lives. It was she who comforted me when my three-year-old son Malachi died from a pestilence that invaded our community, and it was I who helped her prepare Joseph's body for burial.

My respect, my admiration, and my love for her have no limits. I have seen her in moments of great joy and in moments of excruciating pain, and yet she never changes; she stays the same person. She is a humble, quiet, introverted person. Not one to quickly make friends, but one who never rejects a stranger or disappoints a friend. Her greatest quality I would say is her ability to understand, and that ability to understand leads to tremendous compassion. She has a very active and impactful prayer life; one that is very private; and one that is heavily interior; she definitely has a special relationship with God. For me, I can easily understand why Jesus was the person He was, because He was very much like His mother.

In the past three years, Mary and I had several discussions about Jesus, His preaching, and the life He was leading. Our very first discussion about Jesus was at the end of the wedding celebration in Cana. I had observed all that happened, and I knew something very special had occurred. When I asked Mary how Jesus had turned the water into wine, she simply smiled, with a slight hint of pride in her son, and said, "God has seen fit to give Him special gifts." That did not surprise me in the least, as I had often wondered about some of the things Jesus had done as a child and young man. I asked her who these men who were traveling with Him were. They did not look particularly significant. They certainly were not scholars; they had the look of very hard-working men; their clothes were nondescript, and quite frankly, the two or three I had spoken with did not strike me as being particularly bright. Mary smiled more broadly and said that they were important for Him to do the work He had to do.

As Jesus progressed in His ministry, it seemed to me Mary became more concerned about Him. We spoke about this at length, and she explained people are not always open to the truth, especially when they think the truth will in some way hurt them – their status, their power, their ability to direct the lives of others. We had heard reports before of the Pharisees, especially being very angry with Him, and there had been other efforts to have the people turn against Him by someone giving false testimony, but none of those efforts ever came to anything. When I asked her to explain her concern, she was not able to do so. Her concern was based not on facts, but on intuition, on her assumption that power always seeks to maintain itself, even if that means destroying those who threaten it. And Jesus was certainly threatening the established power structures.

When others asked her why Jesus did not respect the Mosaic Law, because He was friends with sinners, tax collectors, and God forbid, Samaritans, Mary would simply smile and say, "Which is more important: the law of man or the law of God?" I finally asked her exactly what she meant when she said that, and she replied that the Mosaic Law was given to Moses so that we could live our lives in a manner pleasing to God. But over time, those laws became ends in themselves, and we live by the law completely forgetting the more important teaching he gave us. I asked, "What teaching is that?" She replied by quoting Deuteronomy, "The LORD is our God, the LORD alone. You shall love the LORD your God with all your heart, and with all your soul, and with all your might." (Deut 6:5) Then she said, "Jesus understands that when you truly love God, you must love all his creation. When you truly love God, it is no sin to save your donkey from disaster on the Sabbath."

It was a few weeks before Passover, after Jesus had been preaching for about three years, when Mary told me she was going to go to Jerusalem to spend Passover with Jesus and His followers. Jerusalem is quite a distance from Nazareth, as she would have to traverse Samaria before reaching Judah and Jerusalem. It was not a trip to make alone, so I told her I would go with her, and she did not object. We needed a male escort, so I convinced my brother Jonas and his son Eldad to take us to the house of Mary of Magdala in Jerusalem. The trip took almost two weeks, and we arrived in Jerusalem the day before Jesus had His triumphant entry into Jerusalem.

We went to see Jesus as He entered Jerusalem on that small donkey. People were everywhere, on rooftops, in the streets, in their doorways, and at every corner. They were normally loud, but when they saw Jesus, they erupted in shouts of *Hosanna! Hosanna!* This was the greeting for a king, not a preacher or a prophet. Even though we were all very happy to see Jesus, and we shouted with the rest, Mary was quiet, subdued, and to my eye seemed sad, or possibly fearful. I asked her if she was well, and she assured me she was. I did not pursue it any further because who can fully know what a mother is thinking and feeling when she sees her son as the focus of public adulation.

It was only four days later when we heard that Jesus had been arrested and was to be tried. We were unable to get access to the Praetorium where He was being tried, so we asked others to report to us what was happening. We heard of His trial by the Sanhedrin and then by Pilate and that the crowd chose Barabbas to be set free instead of Jesus. At that time, we knew all was lost. Jesus would be executed. Mary decided she would go to see Him as He left the Praetorium and follow Him on the walk to Golgotha. I and several others did not think it was a good idea and tried to talk her out of going, but she would not accede to our requests. I, and some of her other friends, including Mary of Magdala, Mary the mother of Clopas, and Joseph of Arimathea, accompanied her and waited outside the gate of the

Praetorium. In the late morning, the soldiers came out, guarding the three prisoners carrying their crosses. Jesus was in the back. We were not allowed to be too close, as we were kept several feet behind the line of soldiers, as far away from the prisoners in the middle of the road as possible. Mary gasped as she first saw Jesus, as it was apparent He had been cruelly tortured. I hoped Mary would want to leave and not witness these proceedings, but she insisted on seeing every action in the process that executed her son.

When Jesus fell the third time, Mary hung onto my arm so that she would not fall. She felt some relief when the Centurion ordered the Cyrenian to help Jesus carry His cross. She was very grateful to the stranger, and after he had reached Golgotha and put the cross down, he started walking back down the hill. In doing so, he passed closely by us. Mary reached out and grasped his hand and squeezed it. He was startled at first, then he looked at Mary, saw the look on her face, and it was as if he instantly knew who she was and that she was thanking him. There was no need for words. With tears in his eyes, he nodded his head and continued walking down the hill.

As I stood at the foot of the cross on which her son was hanging, Mary was slumping against John, who was on her left, as I supported her on the right. I remembered my own grief as I watched my young son gasp for breath as he lay dying, and it was Mary who was at my side, who was the pillar that prevented me from falling. As I returned to the present, I saw the soldiers casting lots for Jesus' cloak. Their game was disrupted by Jesus' words of comfort that He was giving to the prisoner beside Him. A slight smile came to her lips as she realized that only Jesus could be so compassionate to another while He was dying on a cross.

When Jesus spoke, the words committing her to the care of John, the reality of his impending death overtook her. Her grief was overwhelming, but there was no loud sobbing, no exhortation of the injustice of it all, just quiet, internal acceptance of what she understood to be God's will. When Jesus said His last words, "…it is finished," I could feel her body stiffen as she tried to control her grief. Then it became loose, and she almost fainted from the emotional pain. Her body started shaking, almost like a person in convulsions, but she held on, squeezing my arm so hard that it left a bruise. John and I wanted to take her away from this place, but she could not move. Her legs were like pillars of stone, firm and upright and unmovable. Finally, John whispered in her ear: "Mother... Mother. We must go." She turned her head, looked at him, nodded so very slightly, took a small step, and John and I supported her as we walked down the hill and returned to Mary's house in Jerusalem.

Chapter 13
The Thirteenth Witness – Lucius the Centurion

The Death of Jesus (Matt 27:45-54)

From noon on, darkness came over the whole land until three in the afternoon. And about three o'clock, Jesus cried with a loud voice, *"Eli, Eli, Lema Sabathani?"* that is, "My God, my God, why have you forsaken me?" When some of the bystanders heard it, they said, "This man is calling for Elijah." At once, one of them ran and got a sponge, filled it with sour wine, put it on a stick, and gave it to Him to drink. But the others said, "Wait, let us see whether Elijah will come to save Him." Then Jesus cried again with a loud voice and breathed His last. At that moment, the curtain of the temple was torn in two, from top to bottom. The earth shook, and the rocks were split. The tombs were also opened, and many bodies of the saints who had fallen asleep were raised. After His resurrection, they came out of the tombs and entered the holy city and appeared to many. Now when the centurion and those with him, who were keeping watch over Jesus, saw the earthquake and what took place, they were terrified and he said, "Truly, this man was God's Son!"

The Testimony of Lucius:

My name is Lucius. I am a Roman citizen by birth, being born into a merchant family in the town of Hadria, which is east of Rome on the Adriatic coast. I am the Roman Centurion who supervised the crucifixion of the man Jesus. It was I who directed His scourging; it was I who commanded the unit of soldiers who escorted Him from the Praetorium to Golgotha; it was I who ensured He carried His cross and got help when He faltered; it was I who commanded the soldiers to drive the nails through his wrists and feet and to secure Him to the cross. I was there until His very last breath, and it was I who supervised His removal from the cross and gave His body to the man called Joseph of Arimathea.

I cannot remember when I did not want to be a soldier, and this desire became a major source of conflict with my family, who believed only mercenaries should be soldiers. Roman citizens should be leaders, not followers. There was no nobler cause than to function in a manner that increased and expanded the glory of Rome, and I did not believe there was a job better suited to that purpose than that of a soldier. Military life had always attracted me, for its discipline, but yes, also for its danger. I certainly did not want to die and had no great desire to kill, but I also wanted adventure and excitement, and most of all, I wanted to be tested to find out my limits, physically, emotionally, and morally, as a soldier and as a man. As I mastered the art of soldiering, that is to say – killing, I achieved rank and greater command responsibility, causing my family's objections to lessen, and they eventually accepted my choice of career.

As a centurion, I command 100 men and can have more assigned to my command if the situation warrants it. I command a battle-ready unit, trained for close-quarter fighting with an enemy. My base organization is the XI Tribune, of the XVI Cohort of the III Legion, assigned to Palestine and North Africa. Palestine is noted for its periodic flare-ups of violence driven by Jewish zealots and by instigators from Syria and Egypt. There was no expectation of any major conflict or battles; consequently, the entire Legion was not fully manned. I only had a total of 84 soldiers under my command instead of the usual 100. Nevertheless, we were still a formidable fighting force, and since there was no fear of invasion by an enemy, we were more than capable of handling any situation that could conceivably arise from the civilian population in Palestine. In this assignment, my responsibilities were primarily security in nature, so we protected key or important facilities; we escorted and protected important government personnel; we maintained order in the streets by preventing mobs from organizing and rioting; and we executed the orders of the governor relative to imprisonment and death sentences.

I first saw the man Jesus when my sub-commander, Marcus Septimus, returned from the place called Gethsemane after arresting Jesus. At that time, Jesus was not restrained, and He seemed to follow willingly and do as He was told. Marcus Septimus marched Him through the crowd in the courtyard of Caiaphas' house, with members of the mob screaming obscenities, saying He was a false prophet and that He should die. The anger and noise coming from the crowd did not seem to disturb Him, as His facial expression – of calm and possibly indifference – never changed. I wondered how he could not be afraid. The soldiers used some force to keep the mob away, and He was led into the building to face the Sanhedrin.

I did not go into the building to witness the trial, being a typical soldier who disdains politics and everything political. Furthermore, anyone with half a brain knew what the outcome from the Sanhedrin would be. The game was rigged, and the man Jesus, prophet or not, would lose. After a couple of hours, Caiaphas' guards escorted Jesus, looking a bit roughed up, but no change in His demeanor, outside with orders for me and my men to take the prisoner to Pilate. I do not take orders from civilians, but Pilate made it plain to me that I should assist the High Priest in any way possible. The crowd was now getting unruly, as some broke through our line to hit Jesus and scream obscenities at Him. We tightened our ranks and began the march to the Praetorium to see Pilate. By the time we got to the Praetorium, more people had joined the crowd, and not all of them seemed to be against Jesus, but the majority certainly was, and for the first time I heard isolated shouts of "Kill Him!" There was something going on here that was much more than the trial of a criminal, and I did not know what it was.

I escorted Jesus into the Praetorium, and Pilate began his questioning. Throughout the trial by Pilate, several things struck me as being very unusual, very different. The first thing was that Jesus had no official defender, no one to explain His case, no one to state His innocence, and no one to plead for mercy. The second thing was that Pilate questioned Jesus directly, and His manner, tone, and approach to their discussion made Him seem more like a defender than a prosecutor. I believe Pilate wanted to release Jesus and tried several times to do just that, but the crowd, responding to the Sanhedrin, would have none of that. The third thing I noticed was that Jesus offered no defense, no explanation of what he did or said, and whether the charges against Him were true or not. The last thing I noticed was that Jesus offered no deference to Pilate. Instead, He treated him as an equal, and Pilate, usually an ego-driven peacock, did not object. Throughout the entire proceedings, Jesus' face did not change; it never wavered from firm resolve to please don't kill me.

I was very surprised when the crowd chose Barabbas. I could not believe my ears. Barabbas was as evil as a man could be, a multiple murderer of innocent men and women, including Jews; yet they chose him instead of a man who preached and healed people.

It was then that things really got difficult for Jesus, and it was then that I changed from bystander and observer to Supervisor of the men and the process who would execute Him. I watched Decimus delivering his lashes across Jesus' back, and I promised myself I would not discipline Decimus for easing up, noticeably to me if not others, in the last 10-15 lashes he delivered. I was unaware of the placement of the thorny bush on His head, but given the temper of the crowd, I decided not to remove it.

As we began the procession to Golgotha, my demeanor and my decisions became purely professional. I had my six largest soldiers armed with sword, spear, and shield lead the procession, ensuring no one would block our way. I had the three prisoners march in single file about 10 feet apart in the middle of two lines of twenty-five soldiers who protected them from any possible invader coming from either side. I covered the rear where I could see everyone in front of me, including most of the crowd.

The distance to Golgotha was less than a mile, yet it took us almost an hour to complete the journey. The prisoners, for obvious reasons, were very slow as they had been beaten and each was carrying a heavy load. Jesus was particularly slow, probably because He had received the worst treatment. He fell three times, and the third time, I had a stranger, who looked to be very strong, help him. Quite frankly, I was surprised He finished the journey at all because it was obvious how weak He was from the torture He had endured. Soldiers are not supposed to think; we only question when the tactical situation requires it, and of course, we never question political decisions. I was anxious for this to be over; actually, I did not want to be there at all, but duty is duty.

As dispassionately as I could, I ordered the soldiers to remove the external cloaks of the prisoners and to align them with the crosses on which they would be placed. The crucifixion site on the top of Golgotha is not very large, and there were ordinary people from the crowd, both sympathetic and less so, watching the final steps, including a few members of the Sanhedrin looking from further back, ensuring they would not be polluted by anything unclean since Passover was soon upon them. The silence was eerie, then suddenly it was broken by a loud ring tone of metal striking metal with force as the first of the spikes was driven through the wrist of Jesus. Surprisingly, He made no cry of pain. The sound repeated itself in intermittent succession as other spikes were driven into the other wrist and feet of Jesus. Per my orders, the other two prisoners were secured to the cross with ropes; they were not nailed like Jesus.

As it became time to erect the crosses of the three prisoners to the upright position, I could see the fear and anguish on the faces and in the eyes of the other two prisoners. Yet, the face of Jesus had not changed. Again, He showed no fear, no hate, and even though His body was racked with pain, no appreciable anguish. His eyes still had that soft look that He had from the beginning. I thought it was a look of acceptance, a look of forgiveness.

As the crosses settled into the foundation holes to keep them upright, there were painful cries from the other two prisoners, but again, nothing from Jesus. As was the custom, each one was offered a drink of a mixture of wine and myrrh, a mild painkiller to reduce the pain they felt on the cross. The two prisoners eagerly drank theirs; Jesus refused. This man was showing a level of courage and strength that surprised me; but most of all, He showed a consistency in His actions—or His refusal to act—since the time He was arrested, that I found admirable. I thought He would make a really good soldier.

Not too long after He was secured on the cross, He spoke His first words: "Father, forgive them, for they know not what they are doing." His father was not there; what father was He calling to? And asking for "them" (us? me?) to be forgiven after all we had done to Him? This was unbelievable! Who does this? Who is that generous? Who is that forgiving? I could not process His words and come to any understanding.

Not too long after this, the prisoner named Gestas accused Jesus in a mocking tone of not being who He said He was. "If you are the Son of God," he said, "save yourself and us." Jesus did not reply because the other prisoner, Dismas, reprimanded Gestas for his hypocrisy in accusing Jesus and then asked Jesus to be merciful to him. Jesus replied that Dismas would join Him in paradise. All these thoughts were flashing through my mind at a furious rate. At first, they confused me, and then my confusion turned to wonder. This man is dying a most agonizing death in a most despicable way for a crime He did not commit, yet He is forgiving a criminal who admits that his sentence is fair according to his crimes. Who is that generous? Who is that loving?

As Jesus pronounced His words of forgiveness, a most unusual darkness covered the land. It was not totally dark, but the clouds covered the sun, and there was no sunlight to be seen. It was not very long after that when Jesus called upon His father, saying, "...into your hands I commend my spirit." And then with His dying breath, He said, "It is finished." As soon as he said this, things happened like I have never seen. A major earthquake occurred, shaking and rattling us and everything on the land, yet none of the crosses fell. There was a loud noise like thunder that made you cringe in fear and dread. It was as if all of nature was screaming in collective pain at the death of this man. I panicked; I was scared; I felt infinitely small and insignificant. I knew at once that this was no coincidence; I knew that this was God telling the world, our world, that He mourned for the death of his son. I heard myself say, "Truly this man is the Son of God."

After things quieted down, I collected my thoughts as I knew my career as a soldier had just come to an end. If I were to be true to myself, then I must find out more about this man—what He said, what He did, and to understand how His teaching applied to me. After all I had seen and experienced, I knew in the depths of my heart that this was not just a man. As soon as possible, I would search out his followers so that I could learn more about this man—who He was and what he taught. Once I made that decision, I suddenly became very calm, at peace. I knew that my life had changed forever and that the Rome I had served and loved would soon become my enemy.

The Burial of Jesus (Mark: 15: 42-47)

When evening had come, and since it was the day of Preparation, that is, the day before the Sabbath, Joseph of Arimathea, a respected member of the council, who was also himself waiting expectantly for the kingdom of God, went boldly to Pilate and asked for the body of Jesus. Then Pilate wondered if He were already dead; and summoning the centurion, he asked him whether He had been dead for some time. When he learned from the centurion that He was dead, he granted the body to Joseph.

Then Joseph bought a linen cloth, and taking down the body, wrapped it in the linen cloth, and laid it in a tomb that had been hewn out of the rock. He then rolled a stone against the door of the tomb. Mary Magdalene and Mary the mother of Joses saw where the body was laid.

Chapter 14
Reflections on these Stories

No ill befalls the righteous,
But the wicked are filled with trouble.
Lying lips are an abomination to the LORD,
But those who act faithfully are his delight.
A prudent man conceals his knowledge,
But fools proclaim their folly.

*— **Proverbs 12:21-23***

T hirteen people, some young, some older, some Jewish, some Roman, some pagan, some male, some female, some supporters of Christ, and some enemies of Christ, all played a role in the passion and crucifixion of Jesus. As you read and hear their stories, you try to retain as much objectivity as you can so that you can understand their experience witnessing or participating in this event, given the individuals they were, the life experiences they had, the goals and purposes they had in life, and their belief in the importance of truth. Of course, you quickly discover that you are unable to maintain objectivity for any length of time because this event is the seminal event of human history. As you read, learn, and understand these thirteen witnesses, you realize how much you are like them, exhibiting and sharing many of their beliefs and behaviors. As you integrate their stories into your personal life, into the things you have done or not done, you get a better understanding of your own strengths and weaknesses because you acknowledge the many sins similar to theirs that you have committed.

Like most people, these witnesses are complex characters, possessing both virtues and vices, strengths and weaknesses, as well as openness to new thinking and prejudices against it. They exhibit a commitment to justice or total indifference to injustice that does not affect them. Are you concerned about injustice in the world? Are you anguished when you see injustice levied on the poor, the marginalized, those who are unable to defend themselves? If you are, then maybe you are a witness to the truth of Jesus Christ. If you are, then do you testify to the truth of His teachings and His message of love for your neighbor as yourself? So, which of the thirteen are you?

Are you Alon, the quiet businessperson, minding his own business, who simply wants to make enough money to look after his family? Do you have Alon's intellectual honesty and personal integrity to question the decisions of approved authority when those decisions do not fit your experience and the facts that you know to be true? Do you go along to get along, or do you pursue answers to get to the truth because you understand that without truth there is no justice, and without justice, there is no peace? When answers to questions are troubling to you, do you seek clarification and understanding, or do you bury them in your memory because you are unwilling or afraid to challenge the status quo?

Or are you Betzalel, the man who had too much to lose? He is a respected member of the community, a political and religious leader, and by all accounts a good man. If he is identified as a sympathizer of rebel causes, he not only loses his status, but he could be arrested and imprisoned as well. So, what do you do when the truth that you believe is being buried, and fighting for it will only cause you pain and significant personal loss? Do you pursue truth and risk losing everything, like Jesus does, or do you choose to keep what you have and hope that keeping quiet and not objecting to lies and injustice will result in personal reward of increased status and power?

Or maybe you are more closely aligned to Machla, the uneducated, inexperienced servant girl whose innocence, curiosity, and basic honesty in trying to understand a complex world and its social structures create problematic situations that she never intended? Machla does not know how to lie; she is honest and straightforward, albeit lacking in tact. She confronts Peter not to embarrass him or get him in trouble, but she does so because her accusation is true. Peter was with the man called Jesus, so why should she not say so? Yet she has a curious mind and wonders why, after the man Jesus is crucified, this coward suddenly becomes brave and preaches in public in direct conflict with both Jewish and Roman law. This transformation attracts her to want to learn more about this man (Peter) and his message because she intuitively understands that something very much out of the ordinary has happened, and that something is very much related to the man Jesus and the manner of His death. Do you allow your mind to question what you see and hear and ask why, the way Machla does?

Or maybe you are more like Peter, fiercely loyal, but very impulsive, quick to act, but very slow to think. Do your good heart and pure intentions cause you to react to situations without thinking, inevitably making matters worse? Are you quick to make promises that you are not able to keep? Do you not listen carefully to ensure understanding of what is being said? Do you control your ego, or does your ego control you? No doubt Peter was a good man, and like the rest of us, he was entirely human, and that humanity includes weaknesses which took him a long time to understand and to force him to change his behavior. Do you learn from your mistakes and not let them make you impotent to make future decisions the way Peter does?

And then there is Kaleb – the blocked learner. Do you have traits similar to those of Kaleb? Do you reject all new information if it does not support your beliefs or fit with your world view? Does your information come only from sources close to you who think like you and share your beliefs? Do you believe that change is inherently bad, especially if it will change, even improve, the status quo with which you are comfortable? Do you put such absolute value on traditional beliefs or on a personal agenda that you see new ideas different from those beliefs as a threat? Or, like the Grand Inquisitor[1], do you see them as some sort of heresy or treasonous belief that will destroy your world? Is your place in society so sacrosanct that you would do anything to preserve it? Even condone and/or perform acts of violence? Do you believe that your beliefs are superior to those who disagree, and that your belief justifies doing whatever is necessary, up to and including violence, to silence their voices? Are you a person who does not try to distinguish fact from fiction?

Are you understanding of and/or sympathetic to Claudia Procula, a member of the Roman aristocracy and the proud wife of the most powerful Roman official in Judea? Although Claudia understood she had a responsible position in Judea, she was not tyrannical in her treatment of servants, and she seemed to have an inquisitive mind that enabled her to appreciate and even admire certain tenets of Judaism. She understood that as a wife and a woman, her influence over her husband was limited, and that this limitation was a fatal flaw that would lead to catastrophic consequences because her husband was often slow to recognize the political storms that raged around him. Was she too tolerant and accepting of the limitations of her power as Pilate's wife? Should she have been more aggressive in getting to Pilate to convince him to make the tougher decision in the pursuit of truth? Did she do as much as she could to change the outcome of the trial, or was she accepting of her impotence as a woman and a wife in achieving change?

We are all taught to obey orders. A Roman soldier, like Decimus, is trained to levels of discipline and obedience that most of us are not. By all measures, Decimus is a good soldier. He obeys orders and executes them completely and effectively. He accepts his training that he is not to question, not to think, only to obey. Yet Decimus' humanity is greater than his training. His training and experience are unable to completely nullify his humanity, and even though he has completed many floggings before, he has the insight to recognize the flogging of Jesus as different, and this insight leads to compassion, a basic virtue of humanity that he was not allowed to have as a soldier when executing his duties. Would you have the courage to reject all that you have been trained to do and to be out of a sense of compassion and ask the one question a soldier never asks – Why? Why am I flogging this man? Why is He sentenced to death? Or would you choose the easier way, blindly follow orders, and continue to live as a robot and never ask why? Never to make the effort to pursue the truth?

Judas is possibly the most hated figure in the Christian world. Historically, Judas is seen and remembered as the worst of all villains, the one who betrayed his friend and master for a paltry 30 pieces of silver. Certainly, Judas committed the awful sin of betrayal, made worse because his betrayal led to the death of the Son of God (the Word made Flesh). The death of Christ has reverberations in human history that are still problematic today; yet His death was essential to Salvation History because without His death there would be no resurrection, and without the resurrection, there is no salvation, as we Christians believe. But because something good comes from an evil and sinful act, that does not diminish the sinfulness of the act, nor does it make it morally good. So, Judas must be held accountable for his heinous act, but let's not stop at the surface of his act of betrayal. Let's delve into his heart, as much as we can, using scripture, logic, and our imagination to see if there was possibly something more to Judas than just greed or envy or plain stupidity. Was Peter's betrayal of Jesus a "lesser" sin than that of Judas? Why is Peter held in esteem and Judas in disdain? Peter is also guilty of betrayal, and he does so after his very strong protestation that he would die rather than betray Jesus. Peter's sin was rooted in fear; fear of punishment; fear of death. Judas' sin was rooted in ego, lack of humility, and faith. He believed he knew more about Jesus' mission than Jesus Himself. A sin of extreme hubris, not unlike that of Adam.

Do we not have something in common with Judas? Have you ever betrayed a friend? Have you ever repeated a story told to you in confidence? Have you ever retold gossip that was hurtful to others? Have you ever lied, whether to avoid responsibility or embarrassment? Have you ever broken your relationship with a friend or family member because of serious differences in your moral/social/political beliefs? Do you reject the truth simply because it does not fit with your personal agenda? If your answer to any or all of these is yes, you can still argue that those "betrayals" that you committed never resulted in something as serious as the death of another. Very true, but sin is sin. The fact is, we have all been guilty, to some degree, of the sin of betrayal, and since we are sinners, like Judas, it should give us some empathy for what he may have been going through. Look into your hearts and consider the moral issues you are conflicted about, and ask yourself, what is the purpose of your decision? Is it to be consistent with the objective moral good? Or is it to choose that which may benefit you personally, like Judas did?

How many people like Veronica do you know? Quite a few, I am willing to bet. There are many truly good and decent people, by any definition, in this world with whom we often interact. Maybe you are one of them. Is your heart filled with love for all you meet, regardless of physical appearance, race, gender, age, religion, and any other external factor? Do you love them not for who they are or what they have, but because they are children of God and have the incarnated spirit of Christ in them? Do you have empathy and compassion for the weak, the marginalized, the outcast? Does your heart scream for justice when faced with the abuse showered on the powerless by the powerful? Do you truly believe that everyone has the right to life, the right to be treated justly, regardless of their status in life or the crime of which they are accused? As individuals, we usually do not have the power to stop acts of injustice, but we do have the power to challenge them; we have the power to collectively say it is wrong; and, like Veronica, we have the power to wipe the face of Jesus. We do so when we show our love and compassion to the downtrodden and the marginalized.

Have you ever had the experience of starting out on a perfectly normal day when events occur which not only change your day, but change the person you are, change the principles you live by, change your worldview, and even change your life? Things like this happen to people every day. Like the person who wins the lottery, or the person who has an accident that leaves him/her disabled, or the person who suffers the unbearable loss of the sudden, unexpected death of a child, a spouse, or a parent. Or the person who is acceptably healthy and is surprisingly notified of extreme illness that is life-ending. Good things happen in our lives, as do tragedies. Sometimes these events make us better; sometimes not so. Simon of Cyrene had such a day. As a stranger in Jerusalem, minding his own business, looking forward to celebrating Passover with his family, he is conscripted by a Roman Centurion to help carry the cross of a convicted criminal. "Why me?" Simon wondered. "For God's sake, get somebody else!" But that was not to be, so Simon grudgingly agreed to do what he was told, not to be cooperative, but fearful of the consequences if he did not. Carrying the cross was hard work, but that was not the problem. The problem was why was this criminal, definitely in pain, so seemingly calm, not stressed, not anxious, and had a manner that was not condemning nor fearful, but one that was accepting and even forgiving? Why was He not in a panic? It was obvious He had suffered extreme pain and torture, to which the blood on His clothes and face testified. How could He tolerate that circle of thorns on his head? Why was He not angry at the Romans and even at me? Simon had no answers for these questions, but when he saw the look of thanks that Jesus gave him when they reached Golgotha, Simon realized he was in the presence of someone that was beyond his experience. How could someone in such pain have the awareness to be grateful for an act performed reluctantly? As he walked home to his family, Simon reflected on what he had seen, what he had heard, what he had done, and more importantly, on what he felt. He slowly realized his life had completely changed; he was not the same man that started the day. He did not yet understand what caused this change, only that he had encountered something or someone that touched his soul. He knew he had to find the reason for this change. Do you have Simon's intuitive understanding of people? Do you reflect on experiences that do not fit your expectations, that are troubling or uplifting? Do you accept truth that you see and feel in the very depths of your being even when there is no obvious reason to explain it?

If you are very lucky, you have or will have a friend like Hannah. A friend who gives and does not demand; a friend whose presence does not require conversation; a friend on whom you can totally depend for advice, emotional support, and total and complete understanding of your pain, doubts, and fears. Hannah and Mary had that rare relationship of perfect friendship that in itself was an example of Jesus' teaching to His disciples to "love one another as I have loved you." Hannah understood intuitively that something was different in Mary's family, that Mary had a burden that only she could bear, and this meant Hannah could be of service best by quietly supporting Mary in her decisions and in her pain. If you learn from Hannah and develop those traits of patience, understanding, compassion, loyalty, and respecting confidences, just maybe you could become the kind of friend that Hannah is.

We are like Dismas every time we beg God for forgiveness or go to confession and receive absolution. For those brief moments, until we sin again, we are prepared to join Christ in paradise. To really be like Dismas, however, requires strength of character that not all of us have. How do you respond to stress, extreme stress, when things go wrong? Especially when you are at fault? Do you plead innocence? Do you blame God, fate, your friends, or your enemies for your predicament? Are you a professional victim? Do you have the humility and the courage to look into the depths of your soul and admit your guilt? Can you be like Dismas and say: "...we indeed have been condemned justly, for we are getting what we deserve for our deeds...'"?

Can you be like David and say from the heart the words David spoke in the 51st Psalm:

"Have mercy on me, God, in your kindness.
In your compassion, blot out my offense.
O wash me more and more from my guilt,
And cleanse me from my sin.

My offenses truly I know them;
My sin is always before me.
Against you, you alone, have I sinned;
What is evil in your sight I have done."

The confessions of David and Dismas were due to very different circumstances, yet both were rooted in absolute humility and had the same results. David was confessing to his personal sins; Dismas was pursuing justice for Christ, not knowing that by doing so, he would be rewarded with salvation for his selfless act of compassion, love, and justice. However, they have two things in common—perfect humility and sincerity of heart. Will you have Dismas' sense of justice when faced with the hate and bigotry of this world? Or will you join the forces of hate and bigotry because it is safer? Do you have a commitment to be true to yourself, to your values, to all that you hold sacred? Do you keep this belief as a core truth of your being, that to betray it is indeed among the worst of sins? Do you question your beliefs when proven facts are in conflict with those beliefs? Do you have the courage to make a change and reject these beliefs because new facts have shown them to be in error? Do you believe in truth, and that once it is attained, it is a treasure that cannot be compromised?

Lucius, the hardened, idolatrous Roman soldier, had the unique quality of asking himself questions to verify what he was seeing and hearing. Lucius' experience as a Roman soldier and Centurion had taught him how to maintain personal integrity while being faithful to his oath to Rome. His ability to self-check facts to ensure they were consistent with his belief and his oath was invaluable in making him the successful professional he was, and it was these qualities that made him stand out above others and enabled him to reach the highly desired rank of Centurion. But Lucius' purpose was not to be promoted or to achieve fame or glory; it was simply to use his talents to their maximum ability, thereby being true to himself. When this self-checking gave him data that was in conflict with his belief, and made him question his oath to Rome, he had to make a choice—a choice that enabled him to still be true to himself. Lucius made that choice; he chose the truth of the data he saw and heard, even though he knew the repercussions to him personally would be devastating. Do you self-check your beliefs? Do you ever ask yourself, "Does this make sense?" Do you choose proven truth over your preferred truth, even when that proven truth upsets your world and makes you, and others, uncomfortable? Lucius chose the proven truth of fact, as seen with his eyes and heard with his ears, and that truth has set him free. Lucius knew his successful career as a Roman soldier was over, and that he would make a choice that would put him in conflict with Rome—that he would become a Christian.

Chapter 15
So What Does All This Mean?

Do not devise a lie against your brother, nor do the like to a friend. Refuse to utter any lie, for the habit of lying serves no good.

— *Sirach 7:12-13*

We are all on a journey, a physical one and a spiritual one. We experience our physical journey in a very visceral way. We see it; we feel it, we touch it, we taste it. Our physical journey is with us at all times, and in many ways, it controls and demands the things we say and do. Our moral values are those that drive us in our spiritual journey to God, those that keep us faithful to the teachings of Jesus. The beliefs we hold, the decisions we make, the behaviors we express are the drivers in how we live our lives, our physical journey. But since the actions we commit in life reflect those beliefs and values in the depths of our being, we live a Christian life when those actions are consistent with the Christian values that are at the core of our being, and we live a non-Christian life when those actions are contrary to Christian teaching.

The lessons 13 Witnesses have taught us are that we are not slaves to the forces that push and pull our physical lives. Rather, we have the ability to control our physical lives, and we can determine for ourselves how to live by rejecting the thesis of the Grand Inquisitor[1] by not being slaves to lies and corrupt forces. We can make decisions based on truth. We now understand that by going through a process of introspective reflection, by utilizing self-checking techniques, and by carefully evaluating facts as they are presented to us, we do not have to blindly accept what we are told. We can discover truth within ourselves when we pursue that truth humbly and sincerely.

We see in the examples of Alon, Machla, Decimus, Simon, and Lucius that often what we see and know to be true does not align with what we are being told or have been told or what we believe. To the person who values truth and who equates personal integrity with pursuing the truth, the action one must take is obvious – (s)he must challenge and question and pursue those answers that fulfill his/her need for truth. To those of us like Betzalel and Kaleb, truth is often an obstacle to the personal goals of wealth, status, and power. Therefore, truth is not only to be ignored but must also be denied and suppressed.

If we believe that the teaching of Jesus Christ is truth, then it logically follows that to live in that truth, we must first know and understand his teaching, and secondly, we must live His teaching. It cannot be a sometime thing—being Christian on Sunday and not being Christian on other days. Living the teachings of Jesus means we make every effort every day to validate and advance His teachings of love, forgiveness, patience, perseverance, compassion, mercy, and justice, because those are His truths. It is a never-ending pursuit of justice, and there can be no justice without truth. Having been baptized and saying you are a Christian, and going to church every Sunday does not make you a Christian. To be a Christian, one must live a life consistent with the teaching of the gospels, consistent with the lessons Jesus taught in His ministry, and so succinctly summarized in Matthew 25:37-40:

> "Lord, when was it that we saw you hungry and gave you food, or thirsty and gave you something to drink? And when was it that we saw you a stranger and welcomed you, or naked and gave you clothing? And when was it that we saw you sick or in prison and visited you?" And the king will answer them, "Truly I tell you, just as you did it to one of the least of these who are members of my family, you did it to me."

This lesson from the mouth of Jesus is direct and straightforward. If you wish to be a Christian, you must serve; you must love those least able to help themselves—the poor, the marginalized, the despised, the foreigner, the widow, and the orphan. To serve them, to love them, is to serve and love Jesus; it is the only way one can truly be a Christian.

Now that you have read the Thirteen Witnesses, you have the experience of understanding how events affect lives. As you put yourself in the role of those thirteen witnesses, you now have a broader and deeper understanding of the crucifixion event from thirteen different perspectives. As a result of this experience, you have made decisions about yourself and your behaviors, based on the degree to which you agreed or disagreed with the actions and decisions of the thirteen witnesses. This decision-making has forced you to take the first step of introspective reflection, as you look deep into yourselves to determine whether you agree or not. As you pursue these reflections honestly and humbly, the degree to which you are walking in the path of Christ becomes evident. As you begin to experience this self-discovery, you have made the first step in improving your spiritual journey as you begin to understand those areas within you that need improvement for you to become a better Christian.

From the minute Adam and Eve sinned, chaos, as a result of sin, was introduced into the world. With their expulsion from Eden, living became extremely difficult on a physical level and much more so on a spiritual level, as salvation—being united with God—was denied to them, and therefore to us as their descendants. From that moment, mankind was assaulted by a deluge of renegade and parasitic demons.[1] Not the satanic demons represented in the art of the Middle Ages or in Dante's Inferno, but the modern demons of hate, greed, selfishness, rage, pride, self-delusion, self-destructive addictions, racial superiority, social and moral alienation, and so many others. This is blatantly demonstrated by the first recorded sin after Adam's and Eve's expulsion—an act of fratricide, the brutal murder of Abel by his brother Cain. However, the Incarnation of Jesus, His ministry, and His passion, death, and resurrection have given us the tools to resist and overcome these demons. The Incarnation has given us a clear path to salvation. The challenge for us is to follow that path and to do so reflectively and sincerely, understanding where we are on the path at any given point in our lives, recognizing the demons that try to control us, admitting the times we have deviated from the path, and not letting our failures stop our effort to be stalwart in our pursuit of the path leading to oneness with God. As Vincent Pizzuto so clearly states:

> "Union with God is not achieved by human efforts to climb the mountain peaks but by Christ's descent into the misty valley of human history. Each of us must walk the interior landscape of the gospel in the solitude of our own hearts, only to realize that as members of Christ's body, we never walk in isolation. We must each find our own way along the path of contemplation, if only to discover Christ is the way. To touch on the gifts of one's deification is to realize the gospels are not ends in themselves but point invariably to Christ within. 'You search the scriptures because you think that in them you have eternal life, but it is they that testify to me.'" (John 5:39)"[4]

So, you now realize that being a true Christian, living or sincerely trying to live a Christian life, is extraordinarily difficult. In fact, it cannot be done successfully by a purely secular person; it can only be done by making every effort to sincerely live a life guided by Christian moral principles, with the full knowledge that God, through his incarnate Son, will support us with the grace needed to survive and overcome the challenges of a very secular world.

Chapter 16
Conclusion

The Lord guides the steps of a man,
And makes safe the path of one he loves.
Though he stumbles, he shall never fall
For the Lord holds him by the hand.

— Ps 37:23-24

T he word "Christian" means one who believes Jesus Christ is the Son of God; and therefore, one who believes in His teaching and who strives to be obedient to that teaching by living his/her life in a manner that is consistent with that teaching. As a Christian community, we do not fully practice, nor have we fully learned, the teachings of Jesus Christ. Our nation, and our world, is in turmoil because, like the ancient Israelites who constantly betrayed the covenant they made with God, so too do we, as Christians, constantly betray our baptismal promises and the commitment we made to walk in His path. We simply do not follow the teaching of "love one another as I have loved you" (John 13:34); "turn from evil and do good; you must seek peace and pursue it" (1 Peter 3:11); "whatever you did for one of the least of these brothers and sisters of mine, you did for Me" (Matt 25:40); "forgive us our trespasses as we forgive those who trespass against us…" (Matt 6:12); and so many others that provide clear guidance on how we should live our lives in order to grow in our personal spirituality and to have a just and peaceful society. Many believe these teachings are very nice to hear in Church but are really naïve and impractical and will not resolve the continuing frighteningly complex issues that have threatened the world from before the birth of Christ. I disagree.

The American Trappist monk and theologian, Thomas Merton, writes in his book *Contemplative Prayer*:

"Let us frankly recognize the true import and the true challenge of the Christian message. The whole gospel kerygma becomes impertinent and laughable if there is an easy answer to everything in a few external gestures and pious intentions. Christianity is a religion for men who are aware that there is a deep wound, a fissure of sin that strikes down to the very heart of man's being. They have tasted the sickness that is present in the inmost heart of man estranged from His God by guilt, suspicion, and covert hatred. If that sickness is an illusion, then there is no need for the Cross, the sacraments, and the Church. If the Marxists are right in diagnosing the human dread as the expression of guilt and inner dishonesty of an alienated class, then there is no need to preach Christ anymore, and there is no need for liturgy or meditation. History has yet to show that the Marxists are right in this matter, however, since by advancing on their own crudely optimistic assumptions they have unleashed a greater evil and a more deadly falsity in man's murderous heart than anyone except the Nazis. And the Nazis in their turn, borrowed from Nietzsche a similar false diagnosis of the Christian's 'fear of the Lord.' It is nevertheless true that the spirit of individualism, associated with the culture and economy of the West in the Modern Age, has had a disastrous effect on the validity of Christian prayer."[5]

Merton has crystallized, bringing to its essence, the problem Christians have in the modern world. We have become the "me" society. Many of us have replaced the Christian goals of love, humility, and working for the common good that are reinforced and enhanced through prayer with new goals, defined by succeeding in the secular world – making more money, getting more power, more status, and more fame, not really caring who we run over in the process.

If you believe you are a Christian and if you wish to live your life in a manner consistent with the teaching of Jesus, then you must first know what Jesus taught and you must reflect on those teachings to ensure that you understand them. By integrating them into your daily life, they will guide you in all the decisions you make personally and professionally. As we reflect on the crucifixion event, we see early in the trial of Jesus that Pontius Pilate asks his facetious question, "What is truth?" (John 18:38). So, Jesus' trial was about truth—the truth of who Jesus was. Was He really the Son of God, or was He just a smooth-talking charlatan and con man? Did He really cure those people He allegedly healed, or were they paid accomplices to His trickery? Or was He a man whose gifts were from the devil and not from God?

We find the answer to this question in Matt 16:15-17 when Jesus asks Peter who He thinks He is. Peter replies that "You are the Messiah, the Son of the living God." Jesus then says: "Blessed are you, Simon son of Jonah, for this was not revealed to you by flesh and blood, but by my Father in heaven." (Matt 16:16). So, the first clue to the truth of who Jesus is, is one of divine revelation that explicitly and unequivocally tells us that Peter knows this truth because it was revealed to him by God the Father. But divine revelation can still be questioned because we only know it is divine revelation because Jesus told us so, and Jesus is the Son of God, incapable of lying, and we know He cannot act in a manner contradictory to His nature.

So, what is it that makes us believe that Jesus is the Son of God and that God is the perfection of truth and therefore is incapable of lying? The answer is faith. There is an enormous gap between man and God in which man, a finite human being, does not and will never have the ability to understand the ways/truths of God on His own. Faith is the bridge between the infinite and the finite, between God and man, and it is through faith that we have certainty that Jesus is the Son of

God and that what He teaches is true. We believe God is truth, and is therefore incapable of lying because He cannot deny Himself.

So, if we start with the premise that we are indeed Christians, that means our faith has enabled us to accept the truth that Jesus Christ is the Son of God, then it follows logically that to maintain our Christian status, we must then make every effort to live our lives in accord with the teachings of Jesus, the Son of God. That means we must obey all His teachings; that to the degree possible, we must walk in His path; and try our best to be an "alter Christus" – another Christ. As human beings, we know we will never do this perfectly as we will repeatedly fall to sin, but we are confident that our success is not in the perfection of the result, but in the sincerity of effort. This theme is echoed in Thomas Merton's Prayer:

My Lord God, I have no idea where I am going.

I do not see the road ahead of me.

I cannot know for certain where it will end.

And, the fact that I think I am following your will does not mean I am actually doing so.

But I believe the desire to please you does in fact, please you. And I hope I have that desire in all that I am doing......[6]

Every day of our lives, we are faced with private and public allegations of tenuous truth. In our world, due to rapidly expanding media technology, baseless accusations and allegations spread at light speed, often destroying innocent people in their wake. When faced with such allegations, we have the obligation to question, to challenge, to gather more information so that we can make an informed decision, the way the witnesses Alon, Machla, Decimus, Simon, Dismas, and Lucius did. We owe it to ourselves as Christians to pursue truth in all we do, to honor Christ who is within us, and to ensure we stay on His path. We honor the crucified Christ by our willingness to not just advocate truth, but also to suffer for it, as evidenced by the sacrifices of the martyrs. We develop the courage and the strength to do this by maintaining a strong prayer life, including the reflective, meditative, discursive, and contemplative prayer on the Gospels. We do not just pray at specific times and in specific places, but we strive to have our very lives, the actions we perform each day, become our continuing prayer. We need to reflect on these teachings by honestly and humbly delving into the inner core of our being, admitting to our strengths and weaknesses, our virtues, and our vices, and allowing the word of God to flow in and through us so that it becomes a part of us. When we have achieved success in doing this, it is only then that we will be able to say we are walking in the path of Christ. Vincent Pizzuto believes Meister Eckhart, a 13th-14th Century Dominican theologian, who taught that for all who truly possess God, the work they do in the world is more genuinely God's work than their own. Meister Eckhart wrote:

> "Now if a man truly has God with him, God is with him everywhere, in the street or among people just as much as in church or in the desert or in a cell. If he possesses God truly and solely, such a man cannot be disturbed by anybody. Why? He has only God, thinks only of God, and all things are for him nothing but God. Such a man bears God in all his works and everywhere, and all that man's works are wrought purely by God – for He who causes the work is more genuinely and truly the owner of the work than he who performs it."[m]

This concept is reinforced in John 15:5:

> "I am the vine; you are the branches. Those who abide in me, and I in them, bear much fruit, because apart from me you can do nothing."

If you now believe it is extraordinarily difficult to be a Christian, you are right. If you believe that God, as a result of the Incarnation—the Word Made Flesh—and the ultimate passion, death, and Resurrection of His Son, has given us guidance for a way of living that is very difficult to achieve under the best of circumstances and impossible to do on our own, you are right. However, God has not left us to our own devices. To meet the challenges of the Christian life, He also gave us the gift of grace, and all we have to do is ask for it. Through the Incarnation, he has given us his Son, and through the death and resurrection of His Son, a lot of help—specifically the continuing flow of grace through the sacraments and the presence and gifts of the Holy Spirit as prophesied in Isaiah 11:1-2:

> "A shoot shall come out from the stock of Jesse, and a branch shall grow out of his roots. The spirit of the LORD shall rest on him, the spirit of wisdom and understanding, the spirit of counsel and might, the spirit of knowledge, and the fear of the LORD."

And Paul tells us in Galatians 5:22-23, He has given us the fruits of the Holy Spirit:

> "By contrast, (to the desires of the flesh), the fruit of the Spirit is love, joy, peace, patience, kindness, generosity, faithfulness, gentleness, and self-control. There is no law against such things."

We receive these gifts to help us in our spiritual journey because we are heirs of Jesus Christ, which we became by virtue of our Baptism. But these gifts do not work autonomously; they work when God provides us the grace to grow in their understanding and to practice them in our daily lives as we reaffirm our commitment to the message and teaching of Jesus Christ. We receive that grace through our prayer—public, personal, communal, and private. It is in the depths of our heart that we encounter God as we contemplate the teachings, He has given us in both the Old and New Testaments. It is in these meditations, when we humbly and sincerely seek to fully understand the messages of the Gospels, that God showers us with the grace we need to learn, to grow, and to change so that we can walk in His path, to truly, fully, and completely be a Christian.

We now understand that our singular purpose in life is to be an "alter Christus"—another Christ. That as Christians we have the responsibility to live our lives to the fullest degree possible in imitation of Him who gave us the gift of salvation. That in imitating Him, we act as He would act, and we do not punish ourselves for our weaknesses and failures as we fall to sin. Rather, we sincerely accept the grace of forgiveness and become more determined to do what he would do, to walk in His path. To help us in that effort, we say the following prayer humbly and sincerely:

Keep Me on Your Path Lord

When I am angry, give me patience;

Keep me on your path, Lord.

When I am frustrated, give me wisdom;

Keep me on your path, Lord.

When I am stressed, give me calm;

Keep me on your path, Lord.

When a loved one disappoints me, give me understanding;

Keep me on your path, Lord.

When my life is turning upside down, give me perseverance;

Keep me on your path, Lord.

When I am confronted with hate, give me love;

Keep me on your path Lord.

When I am lost, give me hope;

Keep me on your path Lord.

When I am happy, keep me balanced;

Keep me on your path, Lord.

When I have achieved success, give me humility;

Keep me on your path, Lord.

When I am complimented, give me gratitude;

Keep me on your path, Lord.

When I am recognized, control my ego;

Keep me on your path, Lord.

No matter what happens to me, Lord; keep me on your path. No success was achieved without your help; and no disappointment, problem, or crisis can be overcome without your help. Keep me on your path, Lord, so that your presence in me will result in everlasting joy. Amen.

Merton gives us an insight into the purity of prayer, and he warns us of the possibility of prayer being corrupted by fanatics. In "Contemplative Prayer," he writes:

"…When prayer allows itself to be exploited for purposes which are beneath itself and have nothing directly to do with our life in God, or our life on earth oriented to God, then it becomes strictly impure. Prayer must penetrate and enliven every department of our life, including that which is most temporal and transient. Prayer does not despise even the seemingly lowliest aspects of man's temporal existence. It spiritualizes all of them and gives them a divine orientation. But prayer is defiled when it is turned away from God, and from the spirit, and manipulated in the interests of group fanaticism."[8]

Chapter 17
Epilogue

There is one whose rash words are like sword thrusts,
But the tongue of the wise brings healing.
Truthful lips endure forever,
But a lying tongue is but for a moment.
Deceit is in the heart of those who devise evil,
But those who plan good have joy.

— Proverbs 12:18-20

The biggest victim of the current technologies that enable instant communication to the world through blogs, podcasts, social media, and other methods of internet broadcast is truth. In previous times, governments, private organizations, and individuals were held accountable for their public statements, especially when those statements were not truthful and were believed and acted upon. Evidence was required to prove the veracity of those statements, and when that evidence fell short, at a minimum, apologies were issued, and sometimes criminal or civil charges were levied. Perpetrators, when found guilty, were sentenced to jail or required to pay compensation to the victim(s).

Although these legal actions can still be taken against offenders today, there are remarkably few, and they do not seem to be an effective deterrent. Some competent and technically astute adults, albeit of questionable character, have made a career of disputing facts proven to be absolutely true by creating scenarios that have no basis in truth and that obfuscate the issue by confusing readers who do not see through their lies or for whom the lie fits more comfortably with their worldview. These persons excel in an Orwellian manner of turning truth into lies and lies into truth. When these obfuscations are released to the world via websites and social media assaults, challenges are raised, and tremendous division occurs among the public, resulting in emotionally charged opposition by polarized groups, a loss of common ground, and no consensus on effective corrective action to resolve the issue or even to attain understanding of the issue.

It should be noted that often, the bottom line for changing truth into a lie is to create social, political, and/or cultural divisions (tribal groups, so to speak), which result in individuals attacking each other in vile ways, up to and including death threats and physical assaults. The bottom line for creating these strong emotional reactions, this chaos, is money. The bloggers, websites, and social media venues that advance polarization on these issues attract readers, and the more readers they attract, the more ads are placed with them, and the more money they make. So, we see individuals and organizations advancing chaos for their own personal financial gain, and their motive for doing so is that deadly sin that pervades our society—greed.

The Grand Inquisitor's [9]comments that lying to the masses would be the new opium that satisfies their angst, their greed, their selfishness, can now be seen as prophecy. He says: *"...one must follow blindly the guidance of the wise spirit, the fearful spirit of death and destruction, hence (they will) accept a system of lies and deception and lead humanity consciously this time toward death and destruction, and moreover, be deceiving them all the while in order to prevent them from realizing where they are being led, and so force the miserable blind men to feel happy, at least while here on earth"*[10]

The sad fact is that many of these professional liars and sowers of chaos believe they are, and will often claim to be, Christian. In truth, they are very far from being Christian because, as the 13 Witnesses taught us, Jesus Christ is the epitome of truth. He teaches messages of peace, not chaos, and messages of love and justice, not hate, bigotry, and division. There can be no peace without justice, no justice without truth, and no truth without love. Such behavior reminds us of Isaiah 59:3 in his teaching that injustice and oppression must be punished:

> For your hands are defiled with blood,
> And your fingers with iniquity;
> Your lips have spoken lies,
> Your tongue mutters wickedness.

Are we heirs to the teaching of the prophets as stated in Zechariah 8:16-17?

> "These are the things that you shall do: Speak the truth to one another, render in your gates judgments that are true and make for peace, do not devise evil in your hearts against one another, and love no false oath; for all these are things that I hate, says the LORD".

Do we believe and accept the scriptures and the perfection of that teaching in the person of Jesus Christ? Are we heirs to the Kingdom of God as given to us by the Resurrected Christ? If your answer is yes to these questions, then how can we attain the goal of salvation if the life we live is in direct contradiction to the teachings of Jesus? How are we Christians if we do not honor His teaching of love, peace, and justice, and live a life in, and of, truth? For the Christian, hate is not an option. The Christian cannot hate, i.e., deny another the fullness of his/her human and civil rights because of their race, ethnicity, religion, gender, citizenship status, or sexual orientation, if they wish to be true to their Christian faith.

In his treatise on Christian Perfection, St. Gregory, Bishop of Nyssa, wrote in the late 4th Century on the importance of truth and peace in the Christian life:

> "He is our peace, for He has made both one. Since we think of Christ as our peace, we may call ourselves true Christians only if

our lives express Christ by our own peace. As the Apostle says, *He has put enmity to death.* We must never allow it to be rekindled in us in any way but must declare that it is absolutely dead. Gloriously has God slain enmity, in order to save us; may we never risk the life of our souls by being resentful or by bearing grudges. We must not awaken that enmity or call it back to life by our wickedness, for it is better left dead.

No, since we possess Christ who is peace, we must put an end to this enmity and live as we believe He lived. He broke down the separating wall, uniting what was divided, bringing about peace by reconciling in His single person those who disagreed. In the same way, we must be reconciled, not only with those who attack us from outside, but also those who stir up dissension within; flesh then will no longer be opposed to the spirit, nor the spirit to the flesh. Once we subject the wisdom of the flesh to God's law, we shall be re-created as one single man at peace. Then having become one instead of two, we shall have peace within ourselves.

Now peace is defined as harmony among those who are divided. When, therefore, we end that civil war within our nature and cultivate peace within ourselves, we become peace itself. By this peace we demonstrate that the name of Christ, which we bear, is authentic and appropriate.

When we consider that Christ is the true light, having nothing to do with deceit, we learn that our own life must also shine with rays of that true light. Now, these rays of the Sun of Justice are the virtues which pour out to enlighten us so that *we may put away the darkness and walk honorably as in broad daylight.* When we reject the deeds of darkness, and do everything in the light of day, we become light and, as light should, we give light to others by our actions.

If we really think of Christ as our source of holiness, we shall refrain from anything wicked or impure in thought or act and thus show ourselves to be worthy bearers of His name. For the quality of holiness is shown not by what we say but by what we do in life."[iii]

Gregory of Nyssa wrote this 2000 years ago and, it seems today, still too many "Christians" do not know what it is to be a Christian, do not understand the requirement to live in the light of Jesus' teaching, and not only do not know how to walk in the path of Christ, but are not even trying.

We have stated that God, our God, is a God of truth, and his expectation is that we, as his disciples, live truthful lives. We understand we may have to explain the degree to which our lives were truthful as we are told in Psalm 96:11-13:

> Let the heavens rejoice and earth be glad,
>
> Let the sea and all within it thunder praise.
>
> Let the land and all it bears rejoice,
>
> All the trees of the world shout for joy
>
> At the presence of the Lord for he comes,
>
> He comes to rule the earth.
>
> With Justice he will rule the world,
>
> He will judge the people with his truth.

Appendix

FROM THE GRAND INQUISITOR NARRATIVE IN FYODOR DOESTOEVSKY'S THE BROTHERS KARAMAZOV

Source: Fyodor Dostoevsky, The Grand Inquisitor, Translated by H.P. Blavatsky,

Seven Treasures Publications, 2009. Pp 7-49.

In Dostoevsky's novel, *The Brothers Karamazov*, the eldest brother, Ivan, who is an atheist, relates an interrogation he imagines between Jesus and the Grand Inquisitor of the Spanish Inquisition to his youngest and most religious brother, Alyosha. This imaginary interrogation takes place in Seville during the Spanish Inquisition (late 16th century) and is told with satirical comments about Western religious beliefs in general and Catholicism in particular. In this meeting, Jesus is arrested as a heretic, and the Grand Inquisitor is his prosecutor. In questioning Jesus, the Grand Inquisitor levies serious charges against him, specifically because he rejected the three offers (temptations) made to him by Satan after his baptism by John the Baptist. The three offers made to Jesus were:

1. The tempter said to him, "If you are the Son of God, command this stone to be transformed into bread." (Matt 4:3)

2. Then the devil took him to the holy city and placed him on the pinnacle of the temple, saying to him, "If you are the Son of God, throw yourself down; for it is written: 'He will command his angels concerning you,' and 'On their hands they will bear

you up, so that you will not dash your foot against a stone.'"
(Matt 4:5-6)

3. Again, the devil took him to a very high mountain and showed him all the kingdoms of the world and their splendor; and he said to him, "All these I will give you, if you will fall down and worship me." (Matt 4:8-9)

The Grand Inquisitor berates Jesus and argues that accepting any one or all three of the temptations would have made mankind's life better, giving humanity the material and emotional support it needed to have a much less painful and chaotic world. He then condemns Jesus for the gravest of sins—giving free will to humanity—claiming that men do not need or should not have the freedom to choose because choices lead to chaos, and the existing world is proof of that.

As the Grand Inquisitor, a former member of the Catholic hierarchy who is now a cynical non-believer, mocks Jesus for the alleged freedom he gave man, he asserts that man does not need or want that freedom. He says man wants to be led and would give up his freedom freely for "bread." He says: *"Know then, that now, and only now, Thy people feel sure and satisfied of their freedom; and only since they have themselves, and of their own free will, delivered that freedom unto our hands by placing it submissively at our feet."*

He further challenges Jesus: *"Wouldst Thou go into the world empty-handed? Wouldst, Thou venture thither with Thy vague and undefined promise of freedom... for never was there anything more unbearable to the human race than personal freedom!"* He continues to say: *"Dost Thou see those stones in the desolate and glaring wilderness? Command those stones be made bread—and mankind will run after Thee, obedient and grateful like a herd of cattle."* (Pg. 22) He completes this first accusation against Jesus by saying: *"Feed us first and then command us to be virtuous!... The fact will remain recorded that Thou couldst, but wouldst not... accept the offer (of bread), thus saving mankind a millennium of useless suffering on earth."* (Pg. 23-24).

He continues his efforts to prove that Jesus was wrong in giving mankind freedom with a series of verbal attacks against Jesus for his folly in giving such a gift to mankind, and makes repeated derogatory and insulting remarks about mankind. He says of mankind: *"No science will ever give them bread so long as they remain free, so long as they refuse to lay that freedom at our feet and say: 'Enslave us, but feed us.'"* (Pg. 24).

And: *"They will also learn they can never be free, for they are weak, vicious, miserable nonentities born wicked and rebellious."* Then he explains why these people, as insignificant as they are, will be grateful for the loss of their free will: *"In our sight and for our purpose, the weak and the lowly are the more dear to us. True, they are vicious and rebellious, but we will force them into obedience, and it is they who will admire us the most. They will regard us as gods and feel grateful to those who have consented to lead the masses and bear their burden of freedom by ruling over them—so terrible will that freedom at last appear to men."* (Pg. 25).

Jesus does not respond to his comments or to any of the charges made against him and makes no comment throughout the interview.

He culminates his attack on Jesus by telling him that he has forgotten that even death is preferable to a free choice between the knowledge of good and evil. This knowledge was not a gift but a burden, one that is beyond all human strength, and to give man such a gift is proof that he (Jesus) does not love mankind and that he wants man to pursue an unattainable goal, resulting in everlasting pain and frustration. Eventually, mankind would understand that and reject Jesus completely because no one who loves could place mankind in such a state of *"greater perplexity and mental suffering"* (Pg 29).

And so, the Grand Inquisitor condemns Jesus for his love, for his gift of free will, for his insistence that the physical sacrifices one makes on earth can be an opportunity to grow in God's love. Having observed the suffering of man and the chaos in the world, the Grand Inquisitor, once a man of faith and defender of the truth of Jesus, rejects the belief that God loves man. He argues that *"one must follow blindly the guidance of the wise spirit (Satan), the fearful spirit of death and destruction, hence accept a system of lies and deception and lead humanity consciously this time toward death and destruction, and moreover, be deceiving them all the while in order to prevent them from realizing where they are being led, and so force the miserable blind men to feel happy, at least while here on earth."* So, his condemnation is complete: Jesus is a fraud. He is not interested in elevating man to be something better than just human; rather, he has given man an impossible task—the choice of free will—which will guarantee man's failure and condemn him to an earthly life of personal terror.

The Grand Inquisitor continues his cynical rant against God by insisting that He, God/Jesus, offers man freedom, which will lead to a life of terror. Therefore, one must reject His truth in favor of lies. He concludes his attack on the personal freedom of men by saying: *"Then we will tell them it is obedience to Thy will and in Thy name that we rule over them. We will deceive them once more and lie to them once again—for never, never more will we allow Thee to come among us. In this deception we will find our suffering, for we must lie eternally, and never cease to lie."* (Pg 25).

Mankind will believe the lies because they are easier to live with, and the lies will satisfy their immediate selfish needs. Unfortunately, the Grand Inquisitor's cynical explanation of the weakness of humankind—that man is willing to become a moral slave to those who will feed him, and will willingly embrace lies of every kind as long as his greed is satisfied—has become eerily prophetic in our modern world as we see this happening across the globe. Dostoevsky's insight into the weaknesses of human behavior has identified a condition to which modern man has become addicted, and which was brilliantly satirized in George Orwell's *1984*: reject truth and believe the lie. A large portion of our modern world has embraced this tyranny: *"Then we will tell them it is obedience to Thy will and in Thy name that we rule over them. We will deceive them once more and lie to them once again—for never, never more will we allow Thee to come among us. In this deception we will find our suffering, for we must lie eternally, and never cease to lie."*

In this narrative that Ivan created, initially to challenge and irritate his saintly brother Alyosha, there are some very dark thoughts about the human race and where we are going, or will choose to go. But it seems many of us have already chosen, or are willing to choose, to pursue those dark paths as they already *"follow the guidance of the wise spirit ... and they have accepted a system of lies and deception that will lead humanity consciously toward death and destruction, and moreover, will deceive them all the while in order to prevent them from realizing where they are being led, and so force these miserable blind men to feel happy, at least while here on earth."* (Pg 25.) It seems Dostoevsky's words from the mouth of the Grand Inquisitor are more prophetic than he probably intended.

Bibliography and Resources

Assorted websites to research Jewish names for men and women and also to identify locations of cities and towns in Palestine at the time of Christ.

Bible Gateway.com

Fyodor Dostoevsky, *The Grand Inquisitor (Excerpt from the Brothers Karamazov),* translated by H. P. Blavatsky, Seven Treasures Publications, 2009.

The Holy Bible Revised Standard Version, Second Catholic Edition, 2001, Ascension Press, West Chester, Pennsylvania.

The Liturgy of the Hours, Vols I – IV, Catholic Book Publishing Corp. New York, 1975.

Thomas Merton, *Contemplative Prayer*, Image Press, 1966.

Thomas Merton, *Praying the Psalms*, Martino Publishing, Mansfield Centre, CT. 2014.

Vincent Pizzuto, *Contemplating Christ, The Gospels and the Interior Life,* Liturgical Press, Collegeville, Minnesota. 2018.

Wikipedia.com.

---

[1] Read the Grand Inquisitor Summary in the Appendix.

[2] Read the Grand Inquisitor Summary in the Appendix.

[3] Vincent Pizzuto, Contemplating Christ, The Gospels and the Interior life, Liturgical Press, 2018, pp 98-103

[4] Ibid, pg. 34.

[5] Thomas Merton, Contemplating Prayer, Image Press, 1966, pp 85-86.

[6] Thomas Merton, The Merton Prayer, sacredstructures.org.

[7] Vincent Pizzuto, Contemplating Christ, the Gospels and the Interior Life, Liturgical Press, 2018, pp 141-142

[8] Thomas Merton, Contemplating Prayer, Image Press, 1966, pg. 93.

[9] Read the Grand Inquisitor Summary in the Appendix.

[10] Fyodor Dostoevsky, *The Grand Inquisitor (Excerpt from the Brothers Karamazov),* translated by H. P. Blavatsky, Seven Treasures Publications, 2009, pg. 46.

[11] Liturgy of the Hours, Second Reading in Office of Readings on Thursday in the 19th Week of Ordinary Time, Vol IV, Pg.106.

www.ingramcontent.com/pod-product-compliance
Lightning Source LLC
Chambersburg PA
CBHW070601180626
46817CB00005B/1934